***"Pillow books were wedding gifts to help newlyweds in their marital relations,"* Meg explained, smiling**

Rick flipped the book open, landing on an erotic painting of a man with his hand inside a woman's kimono, obviously fondling her breast.

Meg gasped when Rick cupped her breast and slid closer to her on the couch. He slowly tugged open her robe, too, just as the picture dictated. He continued to tease her, expose her, making her glad she was naked underneath.

When Rick's hands moved to her thighs, she tensed in anticipation.

"You can often tell a lot from those pictures by the clothes the characters are wearing—"

"Or not," Rick finished for her, sliding one hand onto Meg's hip and using the other to enter her. She let out a groan as his fingers spread her gently. Just as he was about to bring her to a blazing climax, he slowed his pace. "Go on, sweetheart. I love hearing you dive deep into your subject."

Then they eyed the pillow book's next page....

D0198785

Blaze™

Dear Reader,

When I introduced Asian art historian
Megan Michiko O'Malley in my debut
Harlequin Blaze novel *Her Body of Work,*
I knew that she deserved a love of her own.
Caught between her traditional Japanese
childhood and modern American schooling,
Meg doesn't quite know where she belongs.

While handsome Rick Sokol knows that she
belongs in his arms, his conflicted feelings toward
happily-ever-after are colored by his own past.

Though not one to dwell in the past, like any good
historian Meg must look to it for some unexpected
lessons. Added to the mix is an antique book of
erotic Japanese paintings that can either bring
them together or pull them apart.

I hope you get much pleasure from reading Meg
and Rick's story!

Enjoy!

Marie Donovan

P.S. I'd be delighted to hear from my readers. Visit
www.mariedonovan.com to enter fun contests,
find out more about Japanese erotic art and learn
about my upcoming books.

HER BOOK OF PLEASURE

Marie Donovan

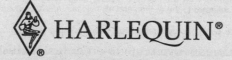

HARLEQUIN®

TORONTO • NEW YORK • LONDON
AMSTERDAM • PARIS • SYDNEY • HAMBURG
STOCKHOLM • ATHENS • TOKYO • MILAN • MADRID
PRAGUE • WARSAW • BUDAPEST • AUCKLAND

ISBN-13: 978-0-373-79306-8
ISBN-10:   0-373-79306-5

HER BOOK OF PLEASURE

This edition published by arrangement with Harlequin Books S.A.

® and TM are trademarks of the publisher. Trademarks indicated with ® are registered in the United States Patent and Trademark Office, the Canadian Trade Marks Office and in other countries.

www.eHarlequin.com

Printed in U.S.A.

ABOUT THE AUTHOR

Marie Donovan is a Chicago-area native, who got her fill of tragedies and unhappy endings by majoring in opera/vocal performance and Spanish literature. As an antidote to all that gloom, she read romance novels voraciously throughout college and graduate school, before writing her own.

Marie has worked for a large suburban public library for the past nine years as both a cataloguer and a bilingual Spanish storytime presenter. She also enjoys reading, gardening and yoga.

Books by Marie Donovan
HARLEQUIN BLAZE
204—HER BODY OF WORK

To my sister Kate:
best friend, brainstormer and
cheerleader extraordinaire

1

"NO WAY. I AM NOT interested." Megan Michiko O'Malley stared at her friend in horror.

"Chicken?"

"I mean it. If you had any kindness in your heart, you wouldn't do that to me."

It wasn't every day Meg saw an elegantly gowned bride cluck and flap her elbows. After one last loud hen imitation, Rey Martinson grinned. "Superstitious, are we?"

"No!" Meg busied herself with shoving the detritus left by the other bridesmaids into one big pile on the vanity table. They could sort out their own lipsticks and eye shadows. "It's only a little bouquet of flowers, not a magic wand to conjure Mr. Perfect."

"There is someone for you, Meg. And he'll probably appear out of thin air when you don't expect him."

Meg rolled her eyes. "It's been so long, I'll probably forget what to do with him."

"Call me if you can't remember." Rey laughed. "But not tonight. It's my wedding night."

"So I guess we have to get you married first." Meg

took a deep breath. She'd just grin and bear it like a good maid of honor. "And then the bouquet toss at the reception."

"Great! Stand in the front row, and I'll throw it straight to you. But watch out for my cousin, Inga. She played field hockey in boarding school."

"Jeez, Rey. Should I get a mouthguard so she doesn't knock my teeth loose?"

"You're much shorter than Inga, so I'll toss it low."

Meg grimaced, picturing herself rolling around on the ballroom floor, pulling hair and clawing with her French-manicured acrylic nail tips. Pro wrestlers would get stomped into the parquet by a crowd of desperate single women at a bouquet toss.

"Promise me you'll *try* to catch the bouquet. I want you to have it." Rey caught her gaze in the mirror, her wide blue eyes pleading.

Meg sighed. It was a waste of flowers, since she had no prospective groom on her horizon. But Rey was in the sappy, syrupy stage of bridal bliss and Meg couldn't pour cold water over her. "I promise."

"Thanks, Meg."

The wedding coordinator popped his head in the door. "Ten minutes, ladies."

Meg checked the back of her friend's gown to make sure the satin buttons were all fastened. "You look beautiful." It was true. Rey Martinson stood almost six feet tall in her strapless white sheath dress. She fit perfectly with what Meg called the three B's: blonde, blue-eyed and big-boobed. Or was that four B's?

Anyway, Meg did love her dearly enough to wedge herself into a bridesmaid dress that she'd only wear today before donating it to the local resale shop. Some short, big-hipped, flat-chested girl would have a great prom.

Unfortunately, Meg's only B's were brunette, big-bottomed and blotchy. She'd inherited her short stature from her Japanese mother and her green eyes from her Irish-American dad. Everything else was a peculiar mix. Her hair was dark brown with reddish highlights, currently pulled into a complicated French twist that matched the bride's. She moved from behind Rey to check her own dress and makeup. "My freckles are still showing," she complained.

"Don't worry. It's not like your mother's here to nag you about them." Rey, of course, had skin like fresh cream thanks to her Swedish heritage.

"She and my father were sorry they couldn't come today. Dad is in the middle of some complicated deal and Mom won't travel outside Japan on her own." Although her traditionally minded mother had taken to the Internet like an *oshidori* duck to water and regularly pecked at her via e-mail.

"Be sure to thank them for the beautiful red silk brocade kimono. The golden embroidery is exquisite."

"It's an *Uchikake* kimono and it's traditionally worn at the wedding reception." Her mother had bought two *Uchikake* kimonos, telling Meg that one was reserved for her. Never mind that Meg hadn't even gone on a date in four months thanks to her teaching schedule at the university. Maybe things would lighten up now that the semester was over.

Rey's mother Brigitte glided into the dressing room on a cloud of expensive French perfume, her beaded silk champagne suit swishing. "Darling, it's time."

Rey stared at her reflection in such a fog of happiness that Meg had to touch her elbow. A wistful ache settled over Meg at how happy her friend looked, preparing to marry the man she loved.

Brigitte kissed her daughter on each cheek and fussed with the spray of tiny white rosebuds in her hair. Meg handed Rey the bridal bouquet, fragrant with large white roses and one pink hibiscus, a tribute to her groom's Cuban roots. Meg grabbed her own smaller bouquet of roses, the pink flowers contrasting nicely against her pale green dress. The color reminded her of a piece of jade in her father's collection and the sash circling her waist looked vaguely like the *obi* that belted a kimono. Rey had a great eye for details, being a wonderful painter and sculptor. She considered keeping the dress, but where on earth would she wear a floor-length green satin dress?

"Thank you for being with me on my wedding day." Rey reached a satin-gloved hand out and squeezed Meg's hand.

Meg opened her eyes wide and blinked to keep the sudden tears from smearing her makeup. "I wouldn't be anywhere else."

"Come, darling, you don't want to keep Marco waiting," Brigitte urged.

"Oh, Mother, Marco's used to waiting for me." She grinned at Meg, who rolled her eyes. Rey got so focused on her art that she often forgot what day it was.

Her mother smiled and kissed her cheek. "He loves you enough to wait for you forever."

Meg followed mother and daughter to the ballroom's threshold, where a string quartet played Vivaldi, waiting for the bride. As Meg stooped to arrange the folds of white satin, Brigitte's words echoed in her head. *A man who'd wait forever?* Ha.

RICK SOKOL was sick of waiting. Waiting for his delayed flight from Hong Kong, waiting on the tarmac for mechanical difficulties, and finally waiting to clear customs at Chicago's O'Hare International Airport. He assured the bored customs officer that he had nothing to declare and slung his battered carry-on over his shoulder.

Double-checking the terminal's huge clock, he set his grandfather's gold wristwatch to central daylight savings time. He'd already missed the six o'clock wedding ceremony, but he'd stop in for the reception. Fortunately, it was at the Palmer House Hilton, where he'd booked a room to crash in once he'd paid his respects to the bride and groom. He'd been awake for thirty-seven hours, thanks to a seatmate who snored loud enough to drown out the jet engines.

He finally fought his way free of the terminal and stepped into the balmy May air, scented with the exhaust of a thousand buses and taxis. The mild temperature was welcome after sweltering through two weeks in Hong Kong. Wearing wires and hidden video cameras under his clothing hadn't helped with the heat, either. But it had been worth it to collect the evidence his client could use in a court case against a company that stole its patented technology.

Flagging a taxi, he collapsed in the backseat and stifled a yawn. "Get me to the Palmer House Hilton in half an hour and there's an extra twenty in it for you."

The driver zoomed away. Rick leaned back, welcoming even a catnap at this point. After he wished the happy couple well, he'd get more sleep at the hotel. Considering his summer to-do list, he'd need all his wits about him.

"CONGRATULATIONS, Marco!" Rick slapped his friend on the shoulder and received an affectionate Cuban bear hug in return. "And how about a kiss from the lovely bride?"

"Tread carefully, *amigo*." Marco narrowed his eyes.

Rick grinned. He and Marco went way back to when Marco was a rookie DEA special agent in L.A. Before meeting Rey, Marco had successfully infiltrated a Caribbean drug cartel as a DEA agent. It had earned him the reputation of a professional badass. Rick didn't often have to use physical force in his own investigations. Intellectual property and corporate espionage cases rarely required muscle, but it was always better to be prepared than wish you had been.

Marco had promised to teach him a few fighting tricks at the gym after he got back from his honeymoon.

Ignoring his friend's mock frown, Rick planted a brotherly kiss on Rey's soft cheek. "I'm sorry I missed the wedding ceremony. I got stuck on the tarmac in Hong Kong and in customs at O'Hare."

"We're happy you made it." Marco gestured to the open bar. "Come get a drink."

"Maybe just one. I've been awake for—" he checked his watch "—thirty-eight hours, and if I have too much I'll fall asleep at the table."

Marco set his empty glass on a passing waiter's tray. "How's the PI biz, Rick? Anything interesting?"

"Some hi-tech companies in L.A. are looking for a new security provider." Rick didn't need to be any more specific. He and Marco both had fairly high clearances to work with defense contractors, especially those involved in weapons and encryption software.

"Excellent." Marco gave him a wolfish grin. "Call me if you need anything. I've been riding a desk for the past couple months."

"Because I didn't want you breaking your leg right before the wedding. Enough shop talk. Rick, would you like to meet some of my single friends?" Rey linked her arm through his and scanned the room. "Meg's here somewhere. Do you like brunettes?"

"Uhh…" The last thing he needed right now was to get involved with anyone.

Marco rolled his eyes. "Don't answer that if you

value your freedom. Ever since we got engaged, she's hell-bent on playing matchmaker."

Rey released him and wrapped her arms around her husband's neck. "I want everyone as happy as we are, darling."

"No one is *that* happy, *querida*." Marco brushed a kiss across his bride's lips. He gazed into her eyes, his expression unguarded and tender.

Rick looked away and rubbed his neck. Their loving glances made him restless. Before he could cover his mouth, he yawned.

"You poor man, dead on your feet and it's only eight-thirty." Rey patted his forearm. "Why don't you go to your room and sleep? We'll be home from our honeymoon in a couple of weeks and we'll take you to dinner."

A hot flush crept up his neck. "Sorry about that. Let me splash some water on my face and I'll be fine."

"Marco says you're staying at your sister's condo while you fix up your grandmother's house for sale. How is your grandma doing?" Rey asked.

"Pretty good. She likes her new assisted living apartment." At least it was still in her familiar neighborhood.

"I'll come over with my tool belt and some beer when I'm back," Marco assured him.

The DJ came over. "Would you like to have the *baile de dinero* now, *Señora* Flores?"

"Yes, Mrs. Flores, it's time for the dollar dance." Marco grinned like a loon at using his wife's married name. "If I have to let my relatives dance with you, at least they can pay for it. And don't let Uncle Armando stuff the money down the front of your dress. That old man needs to remember he's not in a Key West strip club."

"I think I can handle Uncle Armando." Rey smiled demurely.

"I'm sure you can." Marco took her hand and they walked to the center of the dance floor. A long line of eager Cuban men were already waiting for the bride. Marco's line wasn't much shorter, though, with women ranging in age from eighteen to eighty-one.

Rick shook his head and walked toward the men's room.

MEG'S DUTIES as maid of honor were temporarily over. She'd straightened Rey's dress, stood next to her as she'd exchanged her vows and made a witty, yet sentimental toast at the beginning of the sit-down dinner—beef, chicken or vegetarian—taking credit for bringing the happy couple together.

And now that the deed was done and her friend was officially married, Meg sipped at her Cuban sangria and smiled wistfully at the memory of how the bride's and groom's aunts had pinned a pure white lace shawl on the happy couple, a symbol of their eternal connection.

Her own scarlet brocade bridal kimono was no doubt packed carefully away in her mother's lacquer chest. She hoped her mother had used acid-free, lignin-free wrapping paper, because at the rate Meg was going, that kimono would never see the light of day.

Meg slugged down the sangria and clinked the empty cup onto the bar. It must have had more booze than she thought, since she was getting positively maudlin.

And to top it all off, a mascara-hardened eyelash was poking her in the eye. She tried to rub it out but only succeeded in poking her eyeball with an acrylic nail tip. Tears immediately blurred the ballroom's fantastic marbled walls and gold-leafed statuary. She widened her eyes and blinked at the elaborate ceiling mural, hoping gravity would boost her tear ducts' efficiency. Instead, one tear broke free, and the rest followed.

She muttered a curse and headed for the powder room. Rey didn't need to see her maid of honor sobbing into her sangria.

Meg ran down the marble steps and passed a small cocktail lounge. A beefy man in his fifties lurched into her path. She tried to dodge him, but he stomped on her dress anyway.

"Hey, watch it!" she called, but he was already weaving away. She made a noise of exasperation and marched into the powder room. The attendant looked at her strangely and Meg recoiled at her reflection. "Oh, my God, I look like the school slut after prom night."

Huge black rings of supposedly waterproof mascara emphasized the bloodshot whites of her eyes.

Red and green Christmas eyes. Ho, ho, ho. Her long-wearing lipstick had worn off long ago, leaving only a rim of plum lip liner surrounding her pale mouth. Clumps of hair straggled down her cheeks to frame her inkblot freckles.

"Your dress, it is ripped!" The attendant, an older woman dressed neatly in a black dress with white cuffs, approached her. Meg twisted around and groaned. Not only had Drunken Oaf stepped on it and left a shoe print, he had ripped part of the train right off her waist. If it tore any further, the whole Palmer House Hilton would get a frightening view of her ass.

Meg wetted a tissue under the faucet and tried wiping away the raccoon rings of mascara. The damn stuff had finally decided to be waterproof.

Lupe, as her nametag read, *tsked* and pulled out a basket. She arranged a packet of wet wipes, a sample tube of lipstick, a powder compact and a sewing kit. "Come," she commanded, as serious as a surgeon about to make the first cut. "We fix you."

Meg submitted meekly. "Thank you."

Lupe wiped her face with a wet wipe. Meg closed her eyes, relaxing as the cool cloth removed the sticky makeup and drying tear tracks.

Lupe threw away the used wipe and handed Meg the lipstick sample. "We make you pretty for your boyfriend."

"Ha!" The laugh burst out before she could stop it.

"He is the one who makes you sad?"

"No, I poked myself in the eye with my fake fin-gernail." Meg held up the offending digit. "I don't even have a boyfriend."

"Ah." The older woman nodded knowingly.

Meg sighed. "It's not like that. I don't even want a boyfriend. I have a great job at the university, I have a great apartment—well, it's tiny but still very nice—and I have my own life, which my mother refuses to admit because she's still e-mailing me pictures of boring Japanese salarymen who want someone to cook their noodles and watch their children while they get drunk after work."

She took a deep breath, noting how her tirade had brought some color into her cheeks. She applied the plum-colored lipstick sample and smacked her lips.

Lupe brushed at the footprint on the green satin. "All mothers, they want children get married, be happy, find love."

"Find love?" Meg tucked some hairpins into her 'do. "Who said that was necessary for marriage? Not my old-fashioned mother, that's who. Marriage first to a man from a good family, then maybe love. Or maybe not."

"Mothers know best." Lupe threaded a needle with white thread and started stitching Meg's dress. Not wanting to argue with a woman wielding a sharp needle next to her skin, Meg quieted, powdering her freckles until they were almost gone.

Lupe finished mending and snipped off the thread. "All done."

Meg examined the back of her dress in the mirror. Even the footprint was gone. "Wonderful. Thank you so much." She dug in her tiny purse and pressed a bill into Lupe's palm.

Instead of putting the money into her pocket, the older woman gripped her hand, her dark brown eyes earnest. "Listen to your mother. Find a nice man. The old ways are best."

She gritted her teeth. *The old ways.* Her mother used that phrase all the time.

Meg disengaged her hand and barely stopped herself from bowing in farewell. One mention of the old ways and she was falling into the Japanese manners of her childhood. She escaped the powder room, images of Lupe and her mother swirling through her head. She almost heard her mother's voice scolding her as she walked to the wedding reception. Great, now the woman had perfected telepathy. Psychic nagging was even quicker than e-mail.

Lost in her thoughts, she bounced off a blue wall. The wall turned and she saw one of the most handsome men she'd ever seen. No, she corrected herself, not handsome, exactly, but compelling. Magnetic. He had wavy hair with streaks of blond, brown and red all tumbled together, kind of like an old color photo of JFK. His eyes were bright blue with tiny glints of gold, set in sharply angled, tanned cheekbones.

"I'm sorry." His deep voice buzzed across her already jangling nerve endings. She stared at him. He mistook her silence for incomprehension and repeated his apology in careful Cantonese.

"Oh. I'm Japanese, not Chinese." It was nice of him to try, though. How many men apologized in one language, much less two?

"Sorry. I only know a few phrases in Japanese. But one I *do* know is *Hajimemashite*."

Meg tried not to cringe at his accent. "That means 'I'm pleased to meet you.'"

"Exactly." He gave her a white smile, revealing a dimple in one tan cheek. "And I hope you'd say you were pleased to meet me, too."

Meg raised her eyebrows. He certainly was fast on his feet. She wondered if he was fast *off* his feet as well. "I might be pleased to meet you if I knew whom I was meeting."

He extended his hand. "I'm Rick Sokol." She took his hand. Rick's grip was gentle but enveloped her smaller hand. His right wrist was banded by a gold watch that was expensive, but not ostentatious. She wondered if he were a lefty.

He released her hand and she fought a peculiar sense of loss. "What's your name?"

"My Japanese name is Michiko." Where did that come from? She almost never introduced herself to Americans as "Michiko," but she didn't correct herself.

"Mitchy-coe," he repeated, mangling the pronunciation.

Meg giggled, fighting the urge to cover her mouth

like a good Japanese girl. "No, that's not how you say it. It's Mee-chee-ko."

He tried again, getting closer. "Better?" He smiled down at her and her stomach flipped.

She nodded, realizing she was in over her head. She tended to attract either short guys who wanted to tower over her, or pale, weedy types who had seen *Memoirs of a Geisha* twenty-seven times and were fascinated by a Japanese girl with light eyes.

Tall, tanned, gorgeous men did not smile at her like this and ask her a question, which she had totally missed. "Excuse me?"

"I was asking if you're here for a wedding?"

She glanced at her attire and was tempted to reply that no, she always wore green satin dresses around hotel lobbies, like some kinky bridesmaid hooker, but no good Japanese girl would even think that, let alone say it. "Yes, my friend got married this evening."

"Mine, too."

They both glanced at the ballroom and turned to each other. He took a closer look at her, his blue gaze traveling from her face to glide over her bare neck and shoulders. Her nipples tightened and swelled against the snug satin bodice. His blue eyes brightened to an almost cobalt shade, lingering on her breasts. She tottered on her dyed-to-match sandals, a flood of lust washing over her.

Then he grinned. "I thought I recognized that dress. You're one of Rey's bridesmaids."

He'd been checking out the damned dress, not her.

Well, she could at least still be the exotic Michiko. "Yes, I was the maid of honor and Rey's cousins were the bridesmaids. Are you a friend of Marco's?"

"Oh, yeah, we met right after college and have been friends ever since. I'm sorry I missed seeing you at the ceremony, but my flight from Hong Kong was delayed. I just had time to toss my things in my room upstairs and rush down to the reception."

"Hong Kong? You are so lucky—I love Hong Kong." She smiled up at him, remembering days and days spent in the art museum archives examining scraps of calligraphy.

"Have a drink with me and we'll talk about Hong Kong."

"A drink?" She froze midstep and turned. Standing on the fourth or fifth step, she was eye-level with him and the view was even better.

Rick shrugged, his wide shoulders moving elegantly under the well-tailored navy blazer. "To apologize for bumping into you."

How long had it been since she'd had a drink with a hot-looking guy? Too depressing to calculate. "Yes, I'd like to have a drink with you."

"Great." He took her hand and helped her up the stairs as if she were a princess. On the second step from the top, her shoe caught in her hem and she pitched forward.

He caught her against his chest, her feet dangling. Her breath came hard, making her breasts rise and fall against the hard musculature of his chest.

"Are you okay?" At least that's what she thought he said, mesmerized by the movement of his lips.

Her face was inches from his. If she leaned in, she could press her mouth against his to learn how he tasted.

"Michiko?" Real concern deepened his voice.

"I'm fine." She'd be even better if he kept holding her, but that wasn't an option. She loosened her grip on him and slid down his body. It was a long, pleasurable journey. Her breasts scraped against the fine pale blue cotton of his oxford shirt, her nipples peaking. The warmth of his body radiated through her heavy skirt.

"There you go." He steadied her on her feet.

"Thank you." She was so shaken by a rush of desire that she allowed him to fold her hand into the crook of his elbow.

"Marco said the bar would be open during the whole reception." He slowed his long steps to keep pace with her down the corridor into the ballroom. Her tumble into his arms had sharpened her senses to everything, not just him. The gold leaf cherubs on the wall were brighter, the carpet was softer and the chicken dance music had mercifully ended.

Rick guided her to a small table in a corner alcove. "Here we are, Michiko." She shivered, unused to hearing her Japanese name caressed by such a deep, sexy voice. "What would you like me to get you from the bar?"

It had been a long day. "Bushmills Irish whiskey on the rocks."

"You like whiskey?" He was surprised.

She grinned. He probably expected her to order sake or maybe even a mai tai. She couldn't stomach warm rice wine or a fruity umbrella drink tonight. "I drink whiskey sometimes when I'm in America. It's hard to find in Japan." That part was true. Her father had her airmail him two bottles every month. Although Dad wouldn't be caught dead polluting his Bushmills with ice.

"Bushmills it is. I'll be right back." He smiled at her and made his way to the crowded bar through the maze of tables, his movements graceful for such a large man in a small space.

Rick seemed like a nice guy. A sexy guy, too. But appearances were deceiving. Her last relationship the previous fall had seemed promising until Ethan began criticizing every single thing she did. She was too mouthy and not demure enough. Her clothes were too bright and tight. She didn't accept his helpful suggestions.

He should have suggested she call first before coming over. Meg had showed up unexpectedly at his place and found him screwing some Malaysian chick who could barely speak English. Not a problem for Meg, who'd screamed at her in the appropriate Chinese dialect. She'd saved her extensive vocabulary of Anglo-Saxon swearwords for Ethan.

She sighed. Ever since, she'd built up a prickly exterior that was hard to shed, and fighting her way through the Asian art department's tenure committee to get her associate professorship hadn't helped her find her softer side.

"Two Bushmills on the rocks." Rick smiled down at her.

Meg accepted the tumbler as he sat. "You didn't have to get the same drink as me."

"I like whiskey and it's been a while since I drank Bushmills. What should we drink to?" He slipped his arm across her chair, not quite resting it on her shoulders.

"Whatever you'd like." This time she wasn't coy. Every rational thought had fled from her mind at the press of his body against hers. The heat from his body raised goose bumps on her arms.

Rick raised his glass. "To new friends and new experiences." He casually dropped his arm and brushed his fingers over her bare shoulders. She shuddered. His fingertips were only inches from the tops of her breasts. She clamped her thighs together in a futile attempt to relieve the sudden ache.

"You haven't tried your drink." He leaned in, the scent of whiskey mixing with his spicy cologne. His eyes had turned that amazing shade of cobalt again. A lock of wavy hair fell across his forehead as he nodded at her tumbler. "If you don't want it, I'll get something else."

"No, no, this is fine." She sipped, the whiskey warming a path down to her stomach. "So, Rick, what do you do?"

"I own a private investigations company specializing in corporate counterespionage, intellectual property disputes, employee investigations. Basically anything a business owner might need to find out or keep his competitors from learning."

Meg nodded. So he was smart and ambitious. "Corporate counterespionage? Like companies spying on each other?"

"Right. I majored in engineering so I often handle hi-tech cases myself. I was in Hong Kong to investigate a patent infringement case involving this certain piece of technology that—" He cut himself off and grinned. "I must be tired to even tell you that much, and you haven't told me anything about yourself except your Japanese name is Michiko. Do you go by an American name as well?"

Meg grinned back. "Maybe, maybe not. You're the professional investigator, you find out."

"I can find out in thirty seconds if I ask Rey or Marco. Or look in the wedding bulletin."

She shook her head. "That would be cheating. Are you a cheater?" she teased.

His eyes darkened and jaw set. Interesting. "No way." Then his expression lightened. "All right, mysterious Michiko, if you won't tell me, I'll find you anyway. That is, if you do want me to find you after tonight."

She deliberately rested her hand on his, the tiny hairs on the back of his hand tickling her palm. "I do want you. To find me, that is." Her voice came out breathy as she imagined how his fingers would feel touching, caressing her. Maybe tonight? She shivered. He had mentioned his hotel room earlier.

"I will. That's a promise, Michiko."

His sexy voice sliding across her name decided it. Megan O'Malley hadn't had any luck with hot men, so maybe it was time to let Michiko have a try.

And where Michiko went, Meg would come, too. Preferably more than once.

2

RICK WATCHED in fascination as Michiko took a long sip of whiskey.

"That tasted great, warming my throat all the way down." She ran her tiny pink tongue around her pouty lips and stroked the creamy length of her neck, trailing her slim fingers between her breasts. "How was yours?"

"What? Oh. My drink's fine." He'd been distracted by the expression on her face as she caressed her throat and chest. She was the most sensual woman he'd met in a long time, but he would have a hard time finding her if he didn't learn more about her. "Tell me about yourself, Michiko."

"Hmmm, just enough information to give you a challenge. I live in Chicago, but I'm not from here. Rey and I have been friends for a few years."

"Where do you work?"

She laughed. "I'll give you a couple clues. I was born in Japan and I work at a university in the city."

He knew she was as smart as she was beautiful. Was she an artist like Rey? "What department?"

She shook her head, the reddish highlights in her dark hair gleaming. "That's all you get out of me tonight." But her sidelong smile as she sipped her drink told him that wasn't necessarily so.

"You have a drop on the corner of your mouth." He wanted to see her tongue again, watch it make her full lips glistening and wet.

"Can you get it?" She turned her big green eyes on him.

"Sure." Instead of wiping the whiskey with a napkin or even his thumb, he deliberately kissed the corner of her mouth, flicking his tongue over the seam of her lips.

She met his tongue with hers, her taste dark and spicy. Her slender hand rested against his chest, and his heart pounded painfully as if to reach her touch.

He cupped the silken nape of her neck and she moaned, her mouth opening even wider under his. Winding her arms around him, she caressed the hollow of his throat. He planted frantic kisses on her mouth, her cheek and jaw, following the path her fingers had traced, almost down to her breast. Her fingers tightened in his hair and he broke away from her, his heart racing.

They stared at each other and he wiped a shaking hand across his face. "We have to stop."

"Do we?" She lifted an eyebrow.

"What do you suggest?" His pulse pounded painfully.

"I hear the Palmer House has wonderful rooms

upstairs, but I've never seen any." Her eyes were heavy-lidded and seductive, her mouth plump and glistening. "Want to show me yours?"

Oh, boy, did he ever. He pulled his electronic keycard out of his jacket pocket and handed it to her. "I'm in room 1033. I'll meet you in ten minutes." He'd never settle down enough to walk across the lobby if she sat with him. He also didn't want her to be embarrassed if they were caught slipping upstairs together.

She stood and turned to look at him. "Hurry, Rick. I'll be waiting." She wove her way through the tables, her hips swaying in a sinuous stroll.

He tossed back the rest of his whiskey and took several deep breaths. "Believe me, Michiko, I'll make it worth the wait."

MEG MANAGED TO KEEP her walk confident until she got into the empty elevator. The doors glided shut, and she clutched the brass elevator rail.

"What am I doing?" Her voice echoed crazily around the empty elevator, her palm sweaty around Rick's keycard. The mirrored walls reflected someone she'd never seen before. She stepped closer to examine her face. Her eyes were deep green and heavy-lidded, her cheeks flushed. Her mouth was puffy and pink, despite having kissed off all her lipstick. She hoped he didn't have a huge smear of Palmer House Plum on his collar.

She gave a start as the elevator rose. The doors

opened at the ballroom level and the sweet strains of a Nat King Cole love song floated in. A couple staggered into the elevator, kissing and tugging at each other's clothing.

Pretending she was alone was the best course of action. She only hoped they got off the elevator before, well, they got off *in* the elevator.

The redheaded woman was about her age and pulled at the blond man's tie, kissing the bared skin at the base of his throat. "We have to hurry." Her voice was low and feverish.

He grabbed her ass with both hands. "Yeah, I have to get back before my girlfriend notices we're gone."

What a scumbag. Meg braced herself for an explosion of disgust from the redhead.

The woman shrugged. "My boyfriend was dancing with a brunette. I doubt he'll miss me."

The repulsive pair finally stumbled off the elevator onto the ninth floor, one floor below Rick's room.

Well, Nat King Cole might think love was forever, but Meg knew different.

The elevator door opened on the tenth floor. She took a deep breath and followed the corridor to Room 1033. Peeling the keycard off her palm, she jammed it into the slot. It blinked red warning lights.

Good enough. Her foray into anonymous sex was obviously not meant to be. She pulled at the card, but it stuck tight in the slot. Maybe she'd warped the plastic when she clutched it in her hot little hand.

She felt like a burglar, tugging and cursing at the card. She wasn't firing on all cylinders, either, thanks to the Cuban sangria and Irish whiskey.

The card clicked into the slot and the light turned green. Green meant go ahead. Taking a deep breath, she pushed the lever handle.

She fumbled for the light switch and flipped it on. Rick's room was actually a luxurious suite, the elegant living room decorated with heavy cherry furniture. Her heels sunk into the thick blue carpet as she advanced cautiously. The room was immaculate, as if no one were staying here. She passed through a marble-tiled hallway into the bedroom.

At least the bedroom showed some signs of occupation. A carry-on bag that had seen better days lay open on the dresser, a crumpled navy Polo shirt and wrinkled khakis slung over a chair. She peeked into the open bag. Plenty of clean clothes and no sharp weapons, always a good sign. She turned to check the bed, testing the mattress with her hand. Firm but not too bouncy. If she were as casual about sex as she had pretended, she'd shuck off the Jolly Green Midget costume and wait for Rick in bed. Naked. She smiled and she left the bedroom in a hurry.

The glass-walled shower in the huge bathroom was still wet. She sniffed appreciatively, recognizing the citrus-and-sandalwood scent of his cologne. Running her hand over his thick white bathrobe, she took a quick look at the counter, relieved when she didn't find any bottles of antipsychotic medication, jock itch creams, or membership cards for the American Society of Sickos.

Now that Meg was somewhat reassured of her physical safety, she had another horrible thought. What if Rick were married? She considered herself a modern American woman, but she drew the line at married men. A long, thick, indelible line.

She heard a gentle tapping at the door. "Michiko, it's me, Rick."

She froze. No way out now. She hurried to the door and yanked it open. Abandoning any pretense at dissembling, she blurted the question that weighed on her mind. "Are you married?"

"Am I what?" Rick cheered silently. Michiko had come to his hotel room. He leaned over to kiss her and she backed away.

"No, none of that. Not until you tell me if you're married."

"Married?" He straightened. "No, I'm not married. What kind of man invites women to his hotel room if he's married?" As soon as he asked her that, he felt foolish. As part of his investigative training, he'd done infidelity and divorce work. "You're not married, are you?"

Michiko gave him a horrified look. "Hell, no!"

"Yeah, 'hell, no' about sums it up for me, too." He shrugged off his blazer and tossed it on an armchair.

She glanced around nervously, gesturing to the fridge. "Want something from the minibar?"

"No, thanks." His head was still spinning from the whiskey he'd poured on top of his jet lag. "You?"

"No, no." She clasped her hands in front of her, revealing the top curves of her breasts as the dress gaped.

Her vulnerability surprised and touched him. He moved across to her and cupped her shoulders. "Let's go back to the reception. I don't want you to do anything you don't want to."

Although he wanted her badly, he'd wait if need be. He sensed hidden depths to her that he could never fully explore in one hurried night together. And he never could resist a mystery.

She wrapped her arms around his waist and nestled her head against his chest. "I want to stay."

Rick bent to kiss her, and damned if the pull he'd felt in the bar wasn't even stronger. This time, though, he made sure he was the one in control, nipping at her tongue as she tried that roof-of-the-mouth trick again. He plunged his tongue deep into her mouth, mimicking what he planned on doing later. He withdrew his tongue, trying to tease her, but she sucked it hard, holding it tight in her mouth's wet heat. He ground his body against hers, his pants sliding across the fabric of her dress. God, he was almost ready to explode because of a few French kisses.

A twinge in his neck saved him from embarrassing himself. He loved kissing her, but any more action at this angle and he'd need a visit to the chiropractor. Not wanting to contemplate throwing out his back at some crucial point, he straightened. He cupped her adorable face between his palms, her wide cheekbones tapering into a strong chin.

She slowly opened her eyes. "Rick?"

"Come sit with me."

She smiled and pressed a kiss into his palm, her lips warm and tender. "Would you be more comfortable lying down?"

He scooped her into his arms, grinning at her surprised squeal. "I don't know about comfortable, but it'll definitely be more fun."

His long strides took them to the bedroom. He shouldered the door open and carried her inside. The room was pitch-black, so he set her gently on her feet and switched on a lamp in the corner. The maid had turned down his bed, the white pillows gleaming invitingly.

Rick took a deep breath. Despite his uncomfortable erection, he had to take it slow. She was small and delicate, and he wanted to be gentle.

He unzipped her dress, the separation of each tooth buzzing in the darkened silence. A wedge of pale skin appeared as she clutched the bodice to her breasts and looked over her shoulder. He bent to kiss the nape of her neck and she shivered.

"In Japan, the nape is considered extremely sensual." Her voice shook for an instant and she took a deep breath.

"I think I'm going to learn a lot about Japan from you, Michiko." She didn't giggle at his pronunciation this time, so he continued. "What does your name mean?" He brushed his lips over the tender skin on her jaw and circled his tongue around the tiny shell of her ear.

She tipped her head, and he slid his tongue to the top of her bare shoulder. "Beautiful." Her voice came out on a sigh.

"I'm going to show you how beautiful it can be."

She giggled again and turned to face him. "No, my *name* means 'beautiful and wise.'"

"And you are. Your mother must have been psychic."

He thought a shadow crossed her face, but it was too dark to tell. In fact, it was still too dark to see much of anything, so he switched on the desk lamp. Its warm glow turned her skin to gold and her eyes to jade.

His clothes strangled him. He wanted to rip off his shirt, unzip his pants and plunge inside her. *Restraint,* he reminded himself.

He knelt in front of her, rested his fingers over hers, which were still holding the dress. She let go and it slipped. The top slopes of her breasts appeared first, then the dress hung for an instant on her nipples. The bodice fell, baring her to the waist. She moved to cover herself, but he caught her hands and spread her arms wide. He was starving for the sight of her.

"Perfect." Her breasts were small but flawless, the golden flesh crowned with coral nipples. He had to know if she tasted as sweet as she looked, so he leaned forward and sucked her deep into his mouth. She made an incoherent noise and clutched his head against her, threading her fingers through his hair. Her nipple pebbled instantly.

"Mmmm." He swirled his tongue around her areola, exploring the taut flesh. Lifting his mouth, he blew gently on her damp skin. She cried and grabbed his shirtfront.

"No fair! I want to touch you, too." Michiko unbuttoned his shirt with shaking hands. She pushed his shirt off his shoulders and ran her long nails across his chest.

He groaned, falling into her spell again. She laughed and tried to pull him toward the bed, but he didn't plan on letting her take charge. "Not yet." He leaned close and lightly nipped her breast. "You can wait."

"Oh, no, I can't."

He cut off her protest with his mouth, kissing her hungrily until she melted against him. He trailed his lips over her silken skin to her right breast, nuzzling his cheek against her soft flesh. She cupped her breast, offering the nipple to him, and he eagerly accepted, sucking at her with hard, eager pulls.

It was amazingly erotic that almost her whole breast fit into his mouth. He was rapidly developing a preference for small-breasted women, especially when Michiko arched her back and moaned. He shoved her dress off her hips, grabbing her ass with both hands. She rubbed her hips against his bare belly, nearly losing her balance.

"Rick, wait—I have to get my dress." She tugged at his head, making him release her breast. She kicked her feet free and bent over to pick up the dress, her breasts swaying free.

"Forget the dress." He cupped her in his palm, rolling the slick nipple between his fingers.

She closed her eyes and licked her lips, leaning into his caress for a brief second before straightening. "I'll be right there, lover," she said, her husky voice full of promise.

Lover? The word sent a thrill down his spine. He yanked his shirt out of his waistband and threw it on the floor.

Michiko sashayed to the armchair sitting in the corner and draped her dress over it. Her ass was lush and full, barely covered by a tiny pair of pale green panties. Her legs were short and shapely, encased in silky stockings. The stockings were flesh-colored but had some sparkling threads woven throughout. The shimmering lace band of her stockings gripped her thighs only a few inches below her panties.

She slowly bent from the waist to unstrap her high-heeled sandals, showing him where her panties dipped between her buttocks, cupping her folds. He saw a darker green patch where her arousal had dampened the silk. "Stop. I want you to leave the shoes on."

"Do you like tall girls better?" She straightened and lifted an eyebrow.

"Not particularly. I like how the high heels make your breasts jut and your ripe little ass sway when you walk."

She gasped. Then her tongue darted out to moisten her lips and he realized his blunt words had aroused her. She was in luck if she liked plain speaking, since he was too painfully hard to think of a flowery speech.

Sitting on the edge of the king-size bed, he spread his legs wide and adjusted his cock in his uncomfortably snug pants. "Walk over here to me, Michiko."

MICHIKO. What would Michiko do? Meg stared at him, her pulse and thoughts racing. The ball was in her court. *Put out or get out.* She almost giggled with anticipation. His upper body was heavy with muscle. The reddish hair covering his chest glinted gold in the warm, intimate lamplight, his skin a burnished bronze.

Despite Rick's size, though, she wasn't intimidated. She took a deep breath, thrust out her chest and cocked a hip. No point in playing coy anymore. They both wanted the same thing.

She strutted across the bedroom carpet, making sure to throw an extra wiggle in her walk. His eyes darkened to a dark sapphire blue. She moved past him and sat on the side of the bed. Swinging her legs onto the mattress, she crossed her ankles and leaned on her elbows. He had turned to watch her. "Are you coming, Rick?"

Meg didn't know a big man could move so fast. He made a graceful pouncing move, covering her body with his. She shifted under him, and he groaned. "Do that again." He lowered his mouth to hers and she rolled her hips against his erection. Her satin panties rasped erotically across his hair-roughened belly, his cold belt buckle pressing her thigh.

She grabbed his broad shoulders as he stroked her. "You're dripping wet." He pushed aside the elastic and slipped a long, thick finger inside her. She cried out at the intense pressure stretching her. He added another finger, thrusting them in and out. Soft, gasping moans came from her dry throat as he rubbed his chest against hers, her sensitive nipples catching in his hair.

"You like that, don't you, Michiko?" He circled her clitoris with the pad of his thumb, drawing the satin tight against the cleft of her bottom.

Meg nodded, all rational thoughts flying from her mind.

"Good." He stopped.

"What?" Stopping *wasn't* good, not when she was so close, the tiny nub between her legs sending shudders through her. Rick pulled her limp body to a sitting position and tugged the hairpins from her hair.

She pushed his hands away. "Stop! I have to go back to the reception and my hair will be a mess."

"You seem to have the wrong impression, Michiko." He traced a hairpin down to her breast and circled it around her nipple.

"What wrong impression?" Her breath caught in her throat as he swirled the pin around her other nipple.

"That I'm in a hurry. That this is some ten-minute wedding reception quickie." He spread the metal wide, bending it out of shape.

"Isn't it?"

"No." He caught her nipple in the hairpin's curve

and gently squeezed the ends together. "I plan on taking my time."

"I don't want you to take your time." She arched her neck and moaned as he pinched her a bit harder and licked the swollen flesh. "I want to come." She was begging. She never begged during sex. Sex with her ex had certainly not been anything to beg for. Except maybe mentally begging him to finish.

"You will come. But not yet." He released the hairpin and she bit off an unladylike curse. "I want to see your black hair spread over my white pillow. I want to run my hands through it as I pound into you."

Wow. When he put it like that... Meg yanked hairpins out of her French twist and threw them on the floor.

"I said, I'm not in a hurry." Rick pushed her hands aside and ran his fingers through her hair, finding hidden hairpins and setting them carefully on the nightstand. She arched in sheer pleasure as his fingertips massaged her sore scalp.

"Mmmm. Feels good." She rubbed her cheek along the crisp hair of his forearm.

"You look like a little cat when you do that, especially with those green eyes glittering at me." He finger-combed her hair over her shoulders and breasts.

"Do you like little pussycats, Rick?" She peeped coyly at him through the curtain of her hair.

She shrieked as he grabbed her ass and yanked her underneath him, her thighs sprawling wide.

"Pussycats?" His voice was raspy and dangerous as

he eased down her body until his mouth hovered above her stomach. "You have to be careful until you know what they like." He dipped his tongue into her belly button, nibbling at the tender flesh surrounding it.

She giggled and swatted at his head. "Stop! I'm ticklish!" First begging, now giggling. He was certainly bringing out new sides of her in bed.

"There you go. Some pussycats are ticklish. So you have to try something else." He blew on her damp belly and she shuddered, threading her fingers through his thick wavy hair.

"Come here and kiss me." She tugged lightly on his head.

He ignored her command, his stare fixed on her panties. "Do you know what I like to do?" His mouth was so close to her that his deep voice sent vibrations to her clit.

"What?" She let go of his hair.

His blue eyes glowed brightly. All her talk about pussycats had unleashed a tiger. "I love to pet little black pussycats. Pet them and stroke them until they purr."

She gulped.

He yanked her panties to her knees and nuzzled the strip of black hair, his hot breath scorching her throbbing flesh. She mentally blessed Rey for dragging her to the spa for a wax job.

Bikini waxes abruptly flew from her mind as Rick leisurely circled the aching nub with his thumb. She thrashed her head against the pillow, her hips thrusting at him. "Faster, faster."

"Sorry, the pussycat doesn't have a say." He deliberately slowed his caresses to a stop. "Say please, pussycat."

She gritted her teeth and tried to bring her thighs together, but he was lodged firmly between them. He bent and blew on her.

"All right, all right! Please." She rolled her eyes as she said it, making a false show of protest when she was desperate to have him touch her.

He grinned, as if he knew what that bit of submission cost her. "That's better." He ran a finger around her damp opening, lubricating her clit with her own juices. His strokes were hard and fast, stroking her and playing with her. Hard pressure built, tiny pulses wracking her body.

"I must be doing a good job, pussycat, 'cause you're getting all sleek and shiny."

She opened her eyes. His face was only inches from her sex, the black hair glistening with moisture.

He inhaled deeply, his nostrils flaring at the scent of her desire. "Some pussycats love to get wet." He slipped a finger between her drenched folds. "Like you."

"I want you inside me." She tried to tug at him, but he shook his head.

"Not yet." A devilish look crossed his face. "What do pussycats like best?"

"Who cares?" She was burning, crazy to come with his thick cock inside her.

He pulled her panties off, tugging them past her

high heels and spreading her thighs wide. "A nice, long tongue bath."

His hot, wet tongue thrust inside her and Meg cried out. He rubbed his nose over her clit, making her see stars. His mouth worked her relentlessly, lapping at her until she melted.

Waves of pleasure rolled into her belly and breasts. Her heels dug into the sheets, bowing her shoulders into the mattress as she thrashed her head on the soft pillow.

He lifted his face from her and she clutched his head in protest. "Touch your nipples, pussycat."

She obeyed, rolling the stiff peaks between her thumb and fingers, mindless of anything but his lips on her. He lowered his mouth to her clit and sucked her deep, humming vibrating murmurs of pleasure.

"Now who's purring, big guy?"

He grinned at her, his mouth slick. "We're past purring—time for you to scream."

Two of his fingers slipped inside her, filling and stretching her. He flicked his tongue over her clit and pushed his fingers in and out. She ground her hips against his face. The liquid sounds of their passion caught her in a torrent and plunged her over a dark waterfall, her scream echoing to the bottom.

Meg's eyelids were too relaxed to open as she heard Rick go into the bathroom. Every bone in her body had melted into the fluffy bed. She needed something to stiffen her up, and Rick was the man for the job.

RICK WIPED HIS MOUTH on a hotel towel and shed the rest of his clothing before digging into his bag for a condom. He didn't usually go down on a woman the first time he had sex with her, preferring to leave that until they got to know each other's bodies. But it was a night for firsts all around. Michiko responded to him like no one else had, coming with his mouth on her as if they'd been lovers for months, not minutes. He practically sprinted from the bathroom, a strip of condoms dangling from his hand. He skidded to a stop, staring at her exotic, erotic beauty. She had been so tight around his fingers he wondered desperately if he could fit inside her. He ripped open the condom package with his teeth and slid the latex over his penis.

"Wow." Her green eyes were wide.

"I'll be careful, I promise. I'll go slow." He practically babbled in his eagerness to sheathe himself in her.

She spread her legs, showing him her wet pink sex framed with black silky hair. "I'd like it *better* if you go fast."

"*Thank* you." He practically dove on top of her, catching his weight on his forearms just in time to keep from crushing her. Shifting his hips, he sank into her hot depths. She tightened around him, and he had to fight from coming right then. She gave a moan. "Are you okay?"

"Oh, Rick." She twisted under him, her tiny muscles clenching his cock until he wanted to throw back his head and howl. Her sleek legs wrapped around his waist as he plunged and withdrew. He stopped for a second to grab for control and she spiked him in the ass with one of her high heels.

"Ouch!"

"Keep going!"

Served him right for having her wear the sexy shoes to bed. Although he was on top, she tried to take the upper hand. He angled his thrusts, pushing deep and shallow, building her desire then easing her down. He pulled all the way out and brushed the head of his shaft across her moist folds.

She was close to coming again, squirming and moaning despite his teasing. A peach-colored flush spread from her breasts to her face, her mouth gasping and rosy. "More, more."

"Not until you're ready." He slid over her clit, his balls rubbing against the entrance to her slick passage.

She raised her head and bit his nipple.

He reared back in shock, inadvertently driving his cock deep inside her. Locking her legs around him, she lifted her ass and grabbed his balls with her hand.

"Michiko!" He threw away all pretence of finesse and slammed against her. Her hot sheath contracted around him as she rubbed her diamond-tipped breasts against his chest. Her fingers cupped his sac, squeezing and molding him until he swelled and threaten to burst. He gritted his teeth, anxious to get her to climax before he lost it.

He balanced on one forearm and rubbed the swollen nub right above where his body joined hers. She gave a short scream and scratched her nails across his shoulders. He winced, but the stinging sensations spurred a fresh rush of blood to his cock. He fingered her harder and nipped at her neck. She thrashed her head as he licked her earlobe, whispering dark, erotic words into the curve of her ear. "Come hard for me, so my cock can explode in your slick little pussy."

Michiko emitted a wordless cry as she shuddered under him, her tight wetness sucking him in with thousands of tiny pulsations.

He lost control and pounded against her, sinking into a sensual abyss. Just as he was drowning in her mysterious depths, he shattered, calling her name in a long groan. The waves of his orgasm buffeted him until he could hardly breathe.

She held him tight as he gasped for air and collapsed on top of her. The salty scent of sex rose around them. He withdrew carefully, disposing of the condom before he rolled over.

"Rick?" She leaned over him, her thick hair tickling his face. "Are you okay?"

"Mmmm." He pulled her onto his chest, nuzzling her soft neck and breathing in her spicy perfume. "Better than okay."

"Me, too." She rested her cheek on his shoulder. "I'm so glad we did this tonight."

That sounded like she wasn't planning on seeing him again. "Tonight and many more, sweetheart," he emphasized. She'd wrung him dry and he couldn't stay awake any longer. "Need a quick nap." He yawned. "We'll go back to the reception together."

She nodded sleepily. "Back to the reception."

He drifted into oblivion, dreaming of the gorgeous woman he held in his arms.

3

MEG OPENED HER EYES slowly and slammed them shut as the dimly lit room spun. Too much damn sangria and whiskey. What a revolting combination. Having Rick's heavy arm slung across her middle didn't help, either. She eased from under him and pushed up from the king-size bed. He slept on his stomach, limp with exhaustion.

She wished she could hop back into bed with him, sleep all night and wake him with a round of morning nooky. She had to content herself with brushing away the lock of hair that had fallen over his forehead. He stirred at her touch.

She froze as he rolled over, his big body sprawling across the mattress. Her mouth grew dry as the sheet slipped below his belly button, the bulge of his penis outlined in 300-thread count cotton. She wished they could've had more time together, more time for her to fully explore his body, touch all the secret places that drove him wild, drive him over the edge with her mouth.

But there was no time for that, despite how her previously sated flesh quickened at the sight of him.

He reached to where she'd been sleeping and murmured something. Was it her name? He quieted, falling into a deeper sleep.

Her gaze flew to the red numbers on the clock radio. It was 11:00 p.m. She'd been gone for over two hours. Where were her clothes? Okay, her bridesmaid's dress lay on the chair. She wriggled into the wrinkled green thing, which now resembled a wilted lettuce leaf. Yanking the zipper, she stuffed her breasts inside the bodice. Her hair was a disaster. Her tiny purse didn't contain a comb, and she felt weird about borrowing Rick's. Pretty strange, since they'd already done plenty of things more intimate than that.

Her stockings were a write-off too, since Rick had ripped off the elastic bands as he thrust inside her. Her shoes could wait until she got downstairs, but where was her underwear?

Meg scanned the carpet in the dim light cast by the table lamp. Her panties weren't under the crumpled comforter. She tiptoed to the bed, lifting the pillow next to Rick's head. Not there. Short of stripping off the sheet and waking him, she couldn't look anywhere else.

Commando it was. She took a few experimental steps, enjoying how the dress's cool lining rubbed across her bottom and sent a shudder through her.

She'd miss Rick, had never expected to feel such a deep connection to a man she'd only known for a couple of hours. If only they'd met last summer before her disaster with Ethan, when she hadn't been afraid to trust a man. At least she'd been able to drop her guard enough to enjoy herself with Rick.

She turned to gaze at him again as he slept, trying to memorize the breadth of his chest, the soft brownish-red hair that covered his hard muscles.

Who was she kidding? Everything about him was etched in her brain. Would he track her down? Would he even try? All she had to do was tell him her real name and phone number. Or tell Rey to pass her info along.

She shook her head. The ball was in his court now. If she didn't hear from him, either he wasn't interested or she'd console herself that he was a lousy investigator. It wasn't as if she didn't have enough on her plate right now with her career.

She closed the door and walked to the elevator barefoot, her sandals dangling from her fingers. The elevator opened and she got a 200-watt view of herself. If she did have cat's eyes as Rick had said, they now belonged to the cat that had swallowed the canary.

Now she had to sneak into the dressing room and try to do something to wrestle her hair back into submission. She probably also smelled pretty strongly of Rick's cologne. His face had gone some interesting places, she mused, noticing the exact spot in the lobby where she'd bumped into him for the first time. Had it only been a couple hours?

"Look who decided to show her face." The cold Swedish accent grated on Meg. She turned slowly.

"Hello, Inga." Play it casual and then run like hell. The big ones were usually slow on their feet.

The Amazonian blond bridesmaid curled her lip. "Rey's been waiting for you. She said she wouldn't toss the bouquet without her maid of honor."

"Bouquet toss?" Meg felt sick. Her time with Rick had fried her brain, obliterating her promise to Rey in a gigantic blaze of lust.

"Let's go." Inga strode off, taking the steps to the ballroom two at a time, even in her long bridesmaid dress. Meg climbed the other side, not wanting to be crushed into a Swedish pancake if Inga slipped and fell backward.

Meg halted in the ballroom doorway. All the guests had retreated to the edge of the dance floor. Rey stood near the DJ's equipment, casting anxious glances over her shoulder. She caught sight of Meg and beckoned to her. Meg crossed the empty dance floor, her bare feet dragging. Two hundred curious guests stared at her wrinkled dress and mussed hair. Her only consolation was that no one knew she'd left her panties in a suite upstairs.

"Where on earth have you been? And what happened to your hair?" Rey's blue eyes widened. "Who was he?"

"He?" Meg hedged.

Rey leaned close. "You know exactly what I'm talking about. You're missing for over two hours and reappear looking like you rolled out of bed. Whose bed?" She craned her head to scan the male guests.

"Mrs. Flores?" The DJ stood behind her. Rey ignored him. He cleared his throat. "Mrs. Flores, it's time."

Meg rolled her eyes. "He means *you,* Rey."

"Oh." Her friend giggled. "I guess I better get used to that."

"We can do the bouquet toss now that your maid of honor is here." The DJ eyeballed her and grinned, obviously coming to his own conclusions about her late arrival.

"Meg, you stand on the left. I'll aim straight for you." Rey pointed to a spot, and Meg slunk over to take her place with the other single women.

She found herself next to Rey's other cousin Erika, a sweet-faced twenty-year-old with dark blond hair. Erika whispered, "Watch out for Inga. She's been trying to get her live-in boyfriend to propose for over a year. When Rey told everybody that she wanted you to catch the bouquet, Inga got a nasty little gleam in her eye."

"It doesn't matter to me if I catch the bouquet."

"You don't understand." Erika grabbed her forearm. "Seeing Rey get married to a hottie like Marco has pissed Inga off. Ruining the bouquet toss is her bit of revenge."

Inga stood at the other end of the front row, glowering at them. Meg gave her a sugary smile.

"Be careful." Erika melted into the second row.

Meg sighed and tossed her sandals on a nearby chair. She couldn't let Rey's jealous cousin spoil

Rey's plans. Widening her stance slightly, she balanced on the balls of her bare feet.

"Are we ready, ladies?" the DJ hollered over the mike.

A halfhearted cheer came from the crowd. The other women traded uneasy looks at the deadly vibes zinging between the messy maid of honor and the bitchy bridesmaid and faded from hair-pulling range.

Rey glanced over her shoulder to see where Meg stood. She turned to the DJ.

"One! Two!" By "Three!" Inga charged toward Meg like a Chicago Bears defensive linesman.

The bouquet arched over Rey's head, aimed straight for Meg. With one eye on the flowers and the other on Inga, Meg centered her breathing. Inga was almost on top of her, obviously planning to body-check her into next week. Meg turned into Inga's path and grabbed her green satin sash.

Before Meg could step aside and let Inga crash to the floor, Meg slipped on some spilled ice cubes and fell.

Letting the bigger woman's momentum push them both down, Meg rolled onto her back and flipped Inga over her head. The big blonde landed with a thud, her mouth gaping open and closed like a giant *koi* out of water.

Meg leapt to her feet and walked to the battered clump of flowers. An eerie silence fell over the ballroom. She hefted the bouquet high over her head. The guests went crazy, clapping and cheering.

Rey hurried over and scolded her cousin in angry Swedish. Marco laughed so hard he wheezed and had to wipe a tear off his cheek. "Remind me never to get on your bad side. What was that, karate?"

"No." Meg shrugged. "Judo. I studied with my mom's older brother for years."

"Black belt?"

"Only second degree." Meg looked over at Inga, whose failure-to-commit boyfriend helped her to her feet. She figured that it was the blond guy from the elevator. "I never thought I'd need it at a wedding reception."

The DJ announced the garter toss. "By tradition, the winner is the next man to get married. So come on up to get fitted for your ball and chain!"

Several men headed for the exits, only to be corralled by their dates. Despite the DJ's smarmy cajoling, only two extremely natty men sauntered onto the dance floor. Meg took a closer look to see Rey's painter friend Leo and his life-partner Steve. Oh, well. At least Leo or Steve would wear the garter at some social occasion.

"Aaaand…" The DJ smirked at the crowd. "The lucky winner gets to dance with the lovely winner of the bouquet toss!"

Shit, shit, shit! She'd forgotten about that part of this embarrassing tradition. *Leo, Steve, please save me.* But the dance floor filled with men. Men as old as her dad, men barely old enough to vote. Fair-haired men, dark-haired men, but none with wavy brown hair streaked with red and gold. Rick must still be asleep upstairs, dead to the world and fortunately, dead to her humiliation.

Burlesque music blared through the ballroom. Marco winked and tugged Rey to a beribboned chair. The horns played the infamous "stripper" song while Marco ducked his head under Rey's skirt. She squealed and batted at his shoulders, her pale cheeks turning bright pink. After several boom-badda-boom repeats, Marco reappeared with his bride's garter dangling from his teeth. He slingshot the blue lacy elastic into the crowd of guys.

Meg thought women played rough. But men who broke into hives at the idea of dating the same woman for more than three weeks were fighting over the garter as if she were Miss America, Miss November and Miss *Sports Illustrated* swimsuit issue all rolled into one. The thuds of fists on flesh and grunts of pain were audible even over the cheesy music.

The winner popped up from the melee and strutted over to her. The losers glared at him, flexing trampled fingers and stomped toes. One man was helped to his feet after a vicious kidney punch.

"Hi, I'm Pablo, and I can't wait to dance with you." He stood only a couple inches taller than she was, even with his lizard-skin cowboy boots.

"Hi, Pablo." Would this torture ever end? The photographer snapped some gruesome photos. Slow, dreamy music oozed from the speakers and the garter-catcher pulled her against his chest.

Meg stared over his shoulder, determined to avoid eye contact at all costs. It didn't work.

Pablo leaned forward to breathe in her ear. "You must be very comfortable in your own skin."

"What are you talking about?" She pushed away from him.

"You know." His gaze drifted over her body. "Flipping that big chick over your head while you're wearing that fancy dress…and nothing under it."

"Oh, my God!" She'd flashed the wedding guests? "Who else saw?"

He leered at her. "Me and a few friends lucky enough to stand in the right place at the right time."

Meg's stomach roiled. In guy-speak, that probably meant that at least twenty guys had seen her bared to the waist. No wonder they'd been fighting over the garter. They probably thought she was the kind of bridesmaid-gone-wild that would sneak off for a wedding reception quickie. And for the first time ever, they'd be right. But not with anyone but Rick. "I hope you got a good look, because none of you is ever seeing *that* again."

"Too bad. I really dig crazy chicks like you."

"For my friend's sake, I am going to finish this dance with you. Then I will walk away and try to forget I ever met you."

The music ended, and Meg sprinted toward Rey and Marco, determined to say her goodbyes and escape home. At least Marco had been standing across the ballroom in the wrong line of sight. Meg didn't need years of awkward Sunday brunches and Christmas parties.

As if to mock that wish, Pablo came trotting after her. "I'm in room 824 if you change your mind."

"I'd have to *lose* my mind first!" After this evening's festivities, she wondered if she had.

RICK JERKED AWAKE, blinking in the darkened hotel room. Hong Kong? His head cleared and he remembered he was in Chicago. The scent of sex rose from the sheets and he reached out, grabbing a handful of cool satin. "Michiko?"

The satin in his hands was her panties, rumpled and still damp with her musky arousal.

He was alone.

"Dammit!" He threw the panties across the room and cradled his spinning head in his hands. He stood gingerly and flipped the bedside lamp on.

He looked at the clock radio. Almost midnight. He'd been asleep over two hours, but Michiko might still be at the reception. Searching in vain for his discarded briefs, he pulled on a clean pair and threw on his clothes. He took the stairs two at a time to the ballroom and scanned the reception for the petite brunette who had blown his mind. As his eyes were adjusting to the dim light, the happy couple spotted him.

"So where have you been, buddy? Did you fall asleep in the can?"

"Marco!" Rey rolled her eyes. "Don't mind him. He's been drinking Cuban rum all night."

Rick ran his fingers through his messy hair. "I, um, had a drink with one of your friends."

"Really? Which one?"

"Her Japanese name is Michiko." He wanted to ask Rey point-blank for Michiko's full name, but he'd promised not to cheat. He hated cheaters.

"Michiko?" Rey asked him, a big grin on her face.

"Your maid of honor with the exotic green eyes?"

"Ah." Marco nodded. "Her Japanese friend is named…"

"Michiko." Rey elbowed her new husband. "Yes. Michiko left."

"Left?" Rick's euphoric mood plummeted. "Is she staying here at the hotel?"

Rey raised an eyebrow. "She didn't tell you?"

"No."

The DJ needed to talk to Rey, so Rick pulled Marco aside. "Michiko and I made a bet that I wouldn't be able to find her after tonight." It'd be a piece of cake to find her with the clues she'd given him. Then he'd wine and dine her, do things in the right order. He had a pretty good idea what made her tick in bed, but what they had done together was much more than a wedding quickie.

"You? The man who tracked down one of the FBI's most wanted using nothing but his laptop?"

"That guy shouldn't have been peddling my client's new weapons' technology overseas." Rick grinned. "And Michiko doesn't know me that well. Yet."

"Yet. Happy hunting, *amigo,* but be careful. The

Spanish verbs for 'hunting' and 'marrying' sound identical." Marco gave a big laugh and pointed to his tux. "Case in point."

Rey finished her business with the DJ and twirled her new husband onto the dance floor.

Rick watched them spin away, suddenly discontent to stand on the sidelines and observe other people's happiness. Well, no more watching and waiting. He'd waited thirty-two years to meet Michiko and he wasn't going to wait any longer. If he couldn't find a green-eyed Japanese girl at a university in Chicago, he'd better find a new line of work.

4

DRIVING THROUGH the heavy traffic around Midway Airport, Rick couldn't remember the last time he'd shaken off his jet lag so quickly. His evening with Michiko had energized him enough so he'd checked out of the Palmer House early in the morning and dropped his things off at his sister's Lake Shore Drive condo. Fortunately, Cara had also left her SUV for him to use while she spent the summer in Europe.

Although he had plenty to keep him busy over the summer, he really wanted to see Michiko again. The rest of his night had been one long erotic dream, her long black hair pooling on his belly as she lowered her lush mouth to his cock.

He'd woken up sweaty and shaken at that point. To hell with the dream, he wanted the real thing. He had two or three possible hits from his online search, but it was Sunday and the universities were closed. He'd find her soon, he had a hunch. But in the meantime, he'd enjoy his trip to Chicago, starting with an extra-large coffee and fresh-baked *kolackies,* jelly-filled pastries he'd picked up at the European bakery around the corner, even remembering to get a half-dozen prune-filled for his grandmother.

Rick's grandmother Lida Sokol had lived for the past fifty years in the middle-class neighborhood of West Lawn on the South Side of Chicago. She had moved there as a young bride in the post-World War II boom and had never wanted to live anywhere else. Narrow bungalows stretched for miles, fronted by lawns so neatly trimmed they looked like AstroTurf. One guy, spick-and-span in black socks and white sneakers, was using his Shop-Vac to vacuum any maple seeds that dared fall on his grass.

Rick smiled as he remembered tossing papery brown pods in the air, watching them spin like propellers before they speared into the grass. That was before his dad moved them to California, so he must have only been four or five, his little sister three. Old enough to overhear the fighting but too young to understand it.

Now that he was an adult, he didn't see the fun in maple seeds, only the work needed to clean the gutters before they sprouted into a miniature forest.

When had his enjoyment of innocent pleasures disappeared? In fact, his encounter with the mysterious Michiko was the only pleasure he'd found in a long time, and that was far from innocent.

He pulled to a stop in front of his grandmother's bungalow and frowned. The grass was long and frayed around the edges. The lawn service his secretary had hired must have gotten sloppy without anyone on-site riding herd on them. He set the alarm on the SUV and walked to the rusty chain-link gate. Another thing he'd need to have taken care of. His loafers scuffed over the uneven path leading to the tan brick house.

Time to start the renovations and hope the major changes wouldn't upset Grandma. Rick unlocked the worn wooden front door and eased it open, a blast of musty hot air rushing past him. He stepped inside and let the aluminum screen door slam shut.

He surveyed the living room with a sigh. Right out of a magazine—*Good Housekeeping,* 1959. The olive-green carpeting covered what he hoped were hardwood floors. Gold-flocked wallpaper climbed the walls, but the *pièce de résistance* was the plastic couch he remembered from his childhood.

It wasn't really made of plastic, but the harvest gold upholstery had been slipcovered in clear plastic to keep little rugrats like him and his sister from wrecking the fabric. Low-slung and as long as a 1960 Cadillac, it must have not been able to fit in Grandma's new apartment. He'd probably have to dismember it with an ax to get it out the front door.

His cell phone rang, deafeningly loud in the silent house and he checked the caller ID. "Hi, Grandma." She'd been able to keep her same phone number in her assisted living apartment.

"Radek? How did you know it was me?"

He grinned. If the caller ID hadn't given her away, it would have been the fact that she was the only one who called him by his legal name, Radek, the Czech version of Roderick. He gave silent thanks he had been named after his grandfather and not his great-uncles Bohumir and Svatopulk. "My phone shows me your phone number, Grandma. How are you doing?"

"Good, good." Her English was still tinged with a hint of her Czech childhood. "When are you coming to see me?"

He glanced at his watch. "How about noon? That gives me a couple hours here at the house to see what needs fixing, and then I'll take you to lunch."

"You are at the house? At my house?" Her eager voice made him a little sad, but the house had to be fixed up and put on the market by the end of summer before the real estate market dropped off. Leaving it empty for the fall and winter was asking for trouble.

"Yeah, I'm airing it out. Do you need me to bring you anything from here?"

"Hmm." She paused for a second. "I was having a hard time getting up the attic steps, but I think some of your grandfather's things are still there."

"I'll look." At least she hadn't tried the steep stairs. Despite the handrail, he'd almost broken a leg on them more than once.

"Thank you, dear." She waited, unwilling to break their connection.

"Why don't you decide where you want to eat?"

That cheered her up. "I know just the place. That Polish buffet has Sunday brunch with all your favorites—sauerbraten, schnitzel, pierogies…" Grandma rattled off a dozen European delicacies guaranteed to knock him into a calorie-induced coma.

"Sounds great. I'll see you at noon, okay?"

"And don't forget your grandfather's things, Radek."

"No, I won't." After a few instructions on her side and promises on his, he hung up. Time to get to work. He opened a new file on his PDA and started a to-do list. Forty minutes later, his hand was cramping from the several pages he'd entered. His grandparents had maintained the house fairly well but hadn't updated anything. The kitchen was immaculate. And the bathroom had the same pink toilet and tub he remembered, making an eye-popping contrast with the aqua wall tiles.

Rick closed the PDA and wiggled his fingers. How was he going to get everything done? Even if he found someone reliable to do renovations, and that was a big if, the time frame to finish was at least a couple months.

Well, at least he didn't have to live here during construction. Trying to set up a home office in the bungalow's tiny bedrooms would have been tricky with old-fashioned wiring and lack of high-speed Internet, and he often had to work late at night when his Asian contacts were awake.

Not to mention that when he did locate Michiko, he'd want a whole lot of privacy to further their acquaintance. Nothing like waking up to the whine of power tools at 7:00 a.m. to ruin the chance for morning fun. His sister's luxury condo held plenty of possibilities for uninterrupted seduction, like the whirlpool tub, luxurious shower and giant four-poster bed.

But Michiko would have to wait until later. He still had to get those things for his grandmother. He trudged up the narrow attic stairs, hunching over to avoid braining himself on the roof rafters. After his eyes adjusted to the dim light, he wished he *were* unconscious.

Piles of dusty boxes, ancient Christmas decorations and rusty toys crowded the attic floor. Almost sixty years of junk mixed with genuine family mementoes, and he was the one who'd sort it all out, thanks to his dad's recent heart attack and his mom staying behind in California to take care of him.

His sister Cara had offered to come home from Europe, but he'd heard the relief in her voice as he'd assured her he could manage. Her husband had passed away only a few months ago and in her grief, she'd decided to get away from their home and travel overseas.

But he didn't have to dive right in today. He was only grabbing a few of his grandfather's things. A black plastic garment bag hung off a rafter. A suit, maybe? He unzipped it, the sight of brass buttons and brown wool a punch in the gut. His grandfather's army dress uniform hung neatly inside, the insignia and nametag reading "Sokol" still aligned with military precision. When he was a kid, his grandfather had pointed out the different ribbons and medals he'd earned while stationed in post-war Japan.

Rick lifted his favorite medal, the bronze Army of Occupation medal. On the front was a German bridge, but hidden on the reverse like a secret message was an engraving of two Japanese junks sailing in front of Mt. Fuji. Rick had often gone sailing with his family and imagined he was cruising along in front of Mt. Fuji.

On an impulse, he pulled on the jacket, the heavy wool pulling across his shoulders. His grandfather had been only nineteen when he went into the army, still a teenager. When Rick had been nineteen, his biggest concerns were college classes and girls, not necessarily in that order. Grandpa's childhood had been during the Depression, his young adulthood in a hostile, foreign land. He tucked the jacket in the bag before he blew out any seams. The jacket didn't fit in more ways than one.

A large trunk sat nearby. No, not a trunk, a black footlocker stenciled with "Sokol" and an ID number. He lifted the lid and dug through several boxes of yellow airmail letters from Japan addressed to various family members. Lots of photos, too, to make his grandma happy.

On the bottom was a bundle wrapped in some kind of dusty gray cloth. He pulled it out gingerly and unwrapped the rough-woven fabric. It was an old Japanese book, possibly an antique, judging by the thick paper and carved wooden binding. The cover had a picture of some geisha girl prancing along carrying an elaborate umbrella.

He opened the book and almost swallowed his tongue. This time the picture was of a sneering samurai type about to enter a kneeling geisha from behind. The man's penis was ludicrously exaggerated, wider and longer than the woman's arm, like a giant brown mushroom that had sprouted in some creepy fairy-tale forest. "Dream on, buddy," he muttered, dropping into an old wingback chair.

The woman's genitals were as explicit as the man's but were drawn to scale, the red ink emphasizing her inner flesh surrounded by extremely detailed black pubic hair. Both figures still wore their kimonos and had almost blank expressions on their faces.

He flipped from page to page. Elegant Japanese women contorted passionately under fierce warriors. It was a sexual encyclopedia, complete with margin notes in flowing Japanese script. Every exotic position he could imagine plus a couple plain-vanilla missionary positions. Although the Japanese didn't refer to it as missionary position, he supposed irrelevantly.

Some couples made love while jealous maidens watched from behind a screen. One picture was an extremely detailed drawing of a woman's genitals. Another was a picture of a woman lying on a futon cushion. He thought at first she was sleeping, but realized she was pleasuring herself.

The weird pictures combined with his memories of last night got to him. He imagined Michiko, her thick dark hair swirling across his bare skin, her almond-shaped eyes emerald-green with desire.

Michiko on her hands and knees as he plunged into her glistening pink depths. Michiko wrapping her tiny hands around his jutting erection. Michiko pleasuring herself as he watched in secret.

Rick adjusted his hardening dick, a cloud of dust rising from the chair. He blew out a rush of air and rubbed his face. In his several years of investigations, he'd found himself in plenty of unusual, bizarre and even dangerous situations. But nothing could have prepared him for finding antique Asian porn in his grandpa's footlocker.

He heard a car pull up to the house and then the rusty gate squeaked. Grabbing the uniform and strange book, he headed downstairs and set them on the dining table. Through the bay window, he saw his grandmother climb the concrete porch steps. He met her at the door and helped her inside. "Grandma, what are you doing here?"

His grandmother clutched her old black purse, a confused look on her face. Then her gaze refocused on him and she smiled. "Radek! Come here and give me a hug!"

"Hi, Grandma." Rick enfolded her in an embrace, mindful of the birdlike bones of her spine and shoulder under her heavy wool sweater. "It's only eleven o'clock. Did you forget I was picking you up at noon?"

She shrugged. "I wanted to see my house again, so I got a taxi from the senior apartments." She ran her hand over the plastic-covered couch and smiled wistfully.

Rick trailed her through the house as she silently said goodbye. Once the remodeling began, it might be too painful to see her house torn up. Maybe better to remember what used to be instead of trying to adjust to what had to be.

Grandma dabbed her eyes and then gave him a bright smile. "Let's go have a nice lunch, Radek."

He picked up the book and draped the garment bag over his arm to hide it. As they descended the front steps, Betty, the next-door neighbor, came outside to visit. "Lida, so nice to see you! And this is little Radek. Look how he's grown!"

"I go by Rick now," he interjected, but they were already rushing down memory lane, Betty's black bouffant hairdo bouncing as she nodded in response.

"So you're fixing up the place, hon?" Betty patted his arm. He nodded. "Let me know if you need anything. Bob'd be pleased as punch to help you out with any fix-up projects. Tell you the truth, it'd get him outta my hair since he retired from the fire department."

"Will do." Maybe Bob could do some basic remodeling work and keep an eye on the plumbers and electricians. He passed his business card to Betty. "Have him give me a call. And thanks."

"What are neighbors for?" Betty headed back into her house. "Nice to see you again, Lida."

His grandma waved. "You too, um…Betsy."

Betty stopped momentarily, a sad smile crossing her face. Rick gave her a half wave. Grandma had forgotten her neighbor's name after thirty years of living six feet away.

He helped her into the SUV and pulled away from the brick bungalow, identical to dozens in the neighborhood. Knowing what had been upstairs in the attic already made the house look different to him.

The erotic aspects of Japanese culture had taken on a whole new meaning for him since last night. What exactly was that book, and where did his grandfather get it? Rick had to find out.

RICK WATCHED HIS GRANDMA pick at her buffet plate, toying with her favorite pork schnitzel. Even the breaded cutlet hadn't stimulated her appetite. "Eat up, Grandma. Didn't you say your doctor told you to gain a little weight?"

"I know, Radek." She cut a tiny slice and chewed it. He sighed and looked around the crowded Polish restaurant, noticing several tables of young people taking their elderly grandparents out to eat.

Were they having the same difficulty in dealing with his role reversal? For years, Grandma had cared for him, and now he needed to care for her. He didn't resent his new responsibilities but wished it weren't so. She ate more pork and he smiled encouragingly as if she were a child.

He drank the rest of his coffee and watched her nibble a slice of chocolate cake. She finally pushed her plate away and he couldn't delay his questions any longer. "I found Grandpa's army uniform in the attic. What was he like after he came home from Japan?"

"After Japan?" She peered up at him and shrugged. "He left here a boy and came back a man. Bigger, stronger, sure of himself. He came to call on me, and we were married the next year when I turned nineteen."

That hadn't told him much, but what did he expect? Any young man would be changed by military service. And he absolutely drew the line at asking his grandmother about her late husband's sexual prowess.

Suppressing a shudder, he tried another tack. "While I'm going through the house, is there anything in particular you want me to keep an eye out for?"

"Like what?" She eyed him without curiosity. A couple years ago, she would have seen through his investigative attempts and called him on it.

He hated to treat his grandmother like one of his interview subjects, but there was no getting around it. "In the attic. I wouldn't want to throw out anything special, like a present Grandpa brought you home from Japan before you married."

She furrowed her forehead. He only hoped her memory lapses didn't extend back that far. "I remember he gave me a lovely tea set. It's on the shelf in my new apartment. And a lovely lacquer fan. Oh—" Her eyes widened and her cheeks pinkened.

"What?" Was she remembering the book? That

would make almost anybody blush. "Something more personal?"

"Radek!" She tapped him on the forearm, her thin fingers barely registering on his skin. "I don't suppose it matters nowadays since so much has changed for young people. But if my father had found his gift, he would have been very angry. Not at all appropriate back then."

He nodded encouragingly. She continued, "Your grandpa gave me a Japanese robe. It was lovely pink silk with embroidered cherry blossoms and a matching nightgown. A totally unsuitable gift for a man to give an unmarried young lady. I hid it until our honeymoon." She gazed over his shoulder, obviously deep in the past.

"Oh." Rick hid his disappointment. "No books or artwork?"

His grandmother's stare snapped back to him. "Books? Neither of us could read Japanese. And your grandpa wasn't much for art."

He helped his grandmother to her feet and guided her through the restaurant. "No, I suppose not." At least not the art that could be displayed in public.

"HEY, HOW WAS the wedding?" Meg's work-study assistant Holly Burton clumped into her tiny office, the hem of her long-sleeved black dress swirling over battered combat boots. Meg's fancy title of assistant professor of East Asian art history definitely did not come with an equally fancy office.

"Oh, fine, fine." Especially the part she hadn't spent at the wedding. But Holly didn't need to know how fine *that* had been. "Too bad your rock band had a gig at the same time."

"Yeah, it was wild. We were playing in this old warehouse on the west side and the sound was totally awesome. I couldn't hear for, like, six hours after the concert."

"Cool." In Holly's world, temporary deafness was something to brag about.

"Before I forget, I wanted to ask you a favor."

"Uh-huh?" Meg couldn't believe how much crapola had been dumped on her desk. She'd only been out of the office for a week to help Rey with last-minute wedding preparations.

"My friends and I are starting a sorority."

"A what?" Meg looked up from an interoffice memo, printed on paper, urging staff to conserve paper.

"A sorority."

"A sorority?" Holly was the least likely sorority girl in Chicago, with her Goth look and ink-black fingernails.

"You know, where skinny blond chicks all live together, drink cosmos, throw up, binge on Ho Hos, throw up. That kind of thing."

"Yeah, I went to college at the University of Southern California. I can spot 'em a mile away." Just another reason to escape La-La Land.

"Well, we wanted to know if you'd be our faculty sponsor. The stupid university says we can't start a campus group unless we have some adult 'validating our existence.'" Holly made irritated air quotations with her fingers.

"I'm pretty low on the tenure totem pole, you know. I spend most of my time teaching or preparing exhibits instead of publishing scholarly articles." Meg shrugged.

"Everyone loved that Chinese art course you took over last year when Dr. Paxson keeled over during a slide lecture."

The students who had bothered to come to class that day had been either fast asleep or so bored they hadn't noticed their professor had stopped droning ten minutes previously.

Holly plopped into her visitor chair. "Pleeeease, Meg. This sorority is for all the short girls, all the geeky girls, all the girls who don't want to be three percent body fat and ninety-seven percent hair."

"Okay, count me in." In college, she'd been all of the above. "What's your sorority's name?"

"Sweet. Beta Iota Tau Chi."

Meg racked her brain for the bit of Greek alphabet lodged there. "That spells B-I-T-X. Chi in the Greek alphabet is X."

"No, no. B-I-T, then spell out the Chi. *BITChi!* Get it? The university won't realize what we're doing until it's too late!" Holly's brown eyes sparkled.

Meg burst out laughing. It was perfect. "I'm proud to be the faculty sponsor of the *BITChi* sorority. I've always wanted to help mold the next generation of smart-ass women." She would have joined a sorority like that in a second at USC.

"It'll be so cool. Our color is brown plaid and our flower is gonna be the dandelion."

"Let me know if you need me to sign anything." She glanced a rough draft of the exhibition catalog.

"Awesome." Holly headed to her desk but stopped. "By the way, you have an appointment at eleven."

"I do? When did this happen?"

"Some guy called early this morning asking for an art appraisal. He sounded young and cute, so I set him up with you."

"Holly!" Meg massaged her temples. She usually enjoyed her assistant's independent streak, but not today. "Who's it with?" Like it mattered. Young plus cute plus art to appraise didn't usually add up to heterosexual. And any guy would come up short compared to Rick from the wedding reception.

"Sorry, didn't get that part. He said he was bringing in something Japanese."

Meg rolled her eyes and tossed her pen on the desk. "Well, that certainly narrows it down."

"I tried to get some more information, but he didn't want to say over the phone. Could be *manga* comic books, *Hello Kitty* dolls, or a statue of Godzilla for all I know."

"Why didn't Nigel take the appointment?" Nigel Fitzjordan was her boss and notorious for grabbing private appraisal appointments.

"He has a meeting with Dean Stanley to go over

funding for next year. Or as he said, 'a light luncheon at the faculty club to discuss upcoming budgetary concerns.'" Holly did a pretty good parody of Nigel's British accent.

Meg made a face. "Better him than me."

"No kidding." Holly looked around to make sure no other student workers were around. "Speaking of budgetary concerns, I think Nigel's maxing out his credit cards. His assistant says the collection agencies keep calling and leaving messages. He probably spent too much on tweed jackets this month."

Meg fought back a snicker before assuming a stern expression. "Holly…" She pointed toward the door.

"I'm going. You need anything first?"

"Yeah, surf eBay for *Hello Kitty* price comparisons."

CHICAGO UNIVERSITY was only a few miles from his grandmother's house but a world away as Rick passed through a rough section of the South Side. The spires of the university came into sight and he drove through a stone archway into a warren of one-way streets, pedestrian walkways and drop-off lanes. After fifteen minutes of circling, he took the last space in a faculty lot, grabbing the Japanese book as he exited.

He'd made the appraisal appointment first thing in the morning with the closest Japanese art expert he could find, a Dr. Megan O'Malley. Could Dr. O'Malley be his Michiko? He'd read her CV online and her graduation dates showed a woman in her late twenties. And considering Michiko's friendship with artist Rey and her Japanese background, the East Asian art department was a perfect place to find her.

He looked up at the department of East Asian studies, a grim gray stone building that looked as if gargoyles pissed over the side of the roof while a hunchback swung around on a rope. A less likely place to study the lush colors and cultures of Asia he could not imagine. Hopefully Michiko was inside to brighten up the place.

Megan O'Malley was listed in the lobby directory, so Rick climbed the stairs to her office on the top floor. A woman sat at her computer looking at eBay pictures of a fat white cartoon cat, of all things. "Hi, I have an appointment to see Megan O'Malley."

She spun around, looking like a startled raccoon in her heavy makeup. "You're the eleven o'clock appraisal?" Her blood-red lips parted slightly.

"Yes. Are you Dr. O'Malley?" He hoped not. He thought she looked awfully young for an experienced art expert, and she wasn't Michiko.

"Unfortunately, no. I'm Holly, her indentured servant. Summer work-study while she curates an exhibit," she elaborated at his raised eyebrow. "I tried to get hired as coordinator of male nude models, but the woman in the student employment office said if that job were ever posted, she'd apply for it herself."

He laughed. "Maybe you can intern with my friend's new wife. That's her specialty."

"Really? Just like—" The phone rang and Holly

grabbed for it. "Go on in. She's expecting you." The girl gestured to the half-open door.

Nodding thanks, he pushed open the door, but something blocked it. "Hello?"

"I'm coming, I'm coming."

The voice was familiar, low and husky. He heard what sounded like a box being dragged away from the door and tried again. It swung easily this time.

A dark-haired woman bent over a carton of office paper. "Have a seat."

He admired her own seat, nicely outlined in a snug white skirt with orange poppies splashed across it. He'd seen it before wearing a pair of green silk panties he'd found under his hotel pillow. Hot damn. "Hello, Michiko."

She straightened and turned slowly, her green eyes wide in her freckled face. "Rick!"

"Or should I call you Megan?" He grinned. Her Irish name fit her as well as her Japanese name, fiery and spirited.

"You found me." She sat on the edge of her desk, grabbing it for balance.

"I told you I would. And without cheating." He ran a finger down her cheek, her skin just as soft and smooth as he remembered.

She gave him an embarrassed smile. "Look, I was sorry to leave you sleeping, but I had to get back for the bouquet toss. You didn't see that, did you?"

"No, missed the whole thing." Her face was turning pink. "Why, did you catch the bouquet?"

"Oh, yeah. Rey chucked it at my head—I had no choice." She straightened and walked behind her desk, her white high-heeled sandals clicking. God, he loved her in those things and hoped she still had the green ones from Saturday night. "How did you find me?"

"I'm here for an appraisal appointment."

She gave him a puzzled look. "You're my eleven o'clock appraisal? You didn't have to make an appointment—you could have just called me instead."

"I came into some Japanese artwork, and I need an appraisal for insurance purposes. You were actually the closest expert. But if you hadn't been Michiko, I would have kept looking."

"Oh." She sat behind her desk and gestured to the visitor's chair. "Have a seat. But I have to tell you upfront that I'm not an expert in Japanese *manga* comic books, *Hello Kitty* collectibles or post-war porcelain figurines."

"Megan." A knock sounded on the doorjamb. The student worker had a sheaf of papers. "Here are those *Hello Kitty* price comps you wanted."

She shrugged her shoulders and looked sheepishly at him. "Holly, I was joking." Holly left, a grin on her face.

"We don't know each other well yet, so I'll assure you I'm not a big *Hello Kitty* fan."

"I never got that impression." Meg sat back in her chair and gripped the arms, amazed that Rick was actually sitting in her office.

"What kind of impression did you get?" He leaned

forward on her desk, his tanned forearms solid with muscle. "A good one?"

"Um…" Meg tried to look away, but his compelling blue eyes kept her from breaking their glance. "A very good one. You must be an excellent investigator to have found me so fast."

"I'm only fast when I need to be. With certain things, I prefer to take it nice and slow."

If he had been that good in bed with a limited amount of time, what would he do with a whole night? She fought the urge to fan herself and instead extended her hand. "I'm sure you already know this, but my full name is Megan Michiko O'Malley, Ph.D. Pleased to meet you."

He took her hand, but instead of shaking it, he rubbed his thumb across her knuckles. "Radek Karel Sokol, but I'm begging you, please call me Rick. Radek after my grandfather, and Karel after my father, whose name is actually Charles. He decided to rediscover his ethnic roots about the time I was born and gave me a name straight off the streets of Prague."

"Wow, and I thought my name was a mouthful." No wonder he went by Rick.

"Sometimes a mouthful is good." His gaze dropped to her breasts. She shivered, remembering how her breast had fit neatly into his mouth. Her nipples tightened under her thin orange top.

She pulled her hand free and fussed with the orange silk poppy tucked behind her ear, trying to regain her composure. "So what do you have for me to appraise?"

He did some appraising of his own, obviously seeing right through her attempt to regain her equilibrium. He opened his leather carry-on. Whatever he had brought was not large, probably some mass-produced knickknack from post-war Japan. He lifted out a plastic grocery bag and pulled out a square bundle wrapped in dusty gray linen and secured with a rubber band.

The mysterious package intrigued Meg. At least it wasn't some hokey vase or sad-eyed clown figurine.

"It's all yours." Rick set the bundle on her desk.

She pulled off the rubber band and unfolded the cloth wrapper. It was a beautiful hand-painted Japanese pillow book, like those she'd seen only in museums. "Oh, my God." She leaned forward eagerly.

"Yeah, that's what I said when I found it hidden in my grandfather's footlocker from when he was stationed in Japan."

Meg pulled a pair of white cotton gloves over her shaking hands, silently cursing the fact she hadn't yet removed the acrylic nail tips from the wedding. Her palms were sweating and she didn't want to get acidic skin oils on the thick paper. "It's gorgeous. Thick rice paper, which is not made of rice, by the way. It's made of mulberry tree fibers." She glared at him. "And you brought it here in a plastic grocery bag?"

"Sorry, I was in a hurry, and it's pretty musty." He shrugged. "What's the estimate for insurance purposes? I don't know what the market value is for Japanese dirty pictures."

She stiffened. "Dirty pictures? This is an exquisite collection of *shunga,* Japanese erotic paintings. They're clamped together so the paintings can be removed and viewed individually." She demonstrated by taking one out and laying it on the corner of her desk.

"Viewed individually?" Rick leaned forward, the chair creaking under his muscular build. "Ah, for the opportunity to examine all the details up close."

"Sometimes." Meg flipped to the next page and saw a detailed painting of a woman pleasuring herself while her would-be lover watched from behind a paper *shoji* screen. The woman's kimono bared her to the waist as she teased herself with a carved jade sex toy. The man's erection jutted out from his clothing, his hand wrapping around it.

Meg's breath came faster as her nipples tightened against her thin top. Twice since Saturday, she'd done the exact same thing as the woman in the painting, imagining she was with Rick again, pretending he was watching as she touched herself.

"Why else would someone pull out individual pages?" His voice was low, his gaze flicking across her burning cheeks. "Could it be for imagining certain situations? For when someone is alone but has certain wants, certain desires?"

She squirmed against her chair. How did Rick know what she had done in the dark loneliness of her bedroom? Her tongue darted out to moisten her lips. He lifted his ankle to rest on his opposite knee, but not before she saw evidence of his own arousal. It

would be so easy to act on their attraction, to send
Holly on an errand and lock the office door...

A chirping cell phone broke the simmering silence. Rick checked the caller ID display and
frowned. "It's my contact in Hong Kong. I have to
take this call." He flipped open the small silver
phone. "*Ni hao,* Mr. Chen, how are you?"

Meg took a deep breath as he rattled off some
questions. Rick's Cantonese wasn't half-bad. He
didn't butcher it as badly as he did Japanese.

He listened for a few seconds. "Hold on, Mr.
Chen. I'll call you in a minute." Closing the phone,
he walked to the door. "I have to go outside. The reception'll be better."

"Suit yourself. The appraisal might take a while."
She waved a cotton-gloved hand. Now that the dust
from their confrontation had settled, she wanted
some breathing room to regain her composure, as
well as get her mitts on that pillow book.

He placed his hands on her desk and leaned over
until she could see the dimple in his freshly shaven
cheek. "I want more from you than just the appraisal."

"You do?" She couldn't help but look at the naked
couple writhing on the page below them.

His glance followed hers. "I want much, much
more. We're not finished here, Megan Michiko
O'Malley. Book or no book."

MEG SAT IN STUNNED SILENCE after he left. Rick had
met the real Megan O'Malley and hadn't run scream-

ing from the building. Some guys expected a soft, sweet Japanese girl, an effect that she quickly dispelled within a few minutes of conversation. The erotic paintings must have had a powerful sexual effect. She only hoped he wasn't another geisha groupie like her ex, eager to sheathe his samurai sword in any decorative Asian scabbard.

She lost herself in the pillow book's wonderful colors and precise brushwork until Nigel stepped into her office. "Knock, knock."

Speak of the devil. Holly must have sneaked outside for a smoke. She wouldn't have let him slither past. "Hello, Nigel, I'm in a meeting."

He waved a languid hand. "Just popping in to drop off some papers that need your immediate attention."

She tried to casually slip a manila folder over the pillow book, but his beady brown eyes widened. "What is that?"

"I'm doing a quick appraisal for a friend." Her glance traveled to the desk corner where she'd left the painting.

Unfortunately, Nigel saw it too. "My dear, Megan, are you appraising *shunga?*" He grabbed the painting with his bare hands, even sticking his thumb right in the image's center.

She winced and took it away from him. "Yes, Nigel, please be careful." She tucked the painting into the book.

"Quite a fine woodblock print."

He couldn't even tell what it was? Sometimes she

wondered if Nigel had earned his fancy university degree from the British College of Fartington-on-Bullshit. "Actually, it's hand-painted. I'll have to do more research, but I think it must have been commissioned by a collector over two hundred years ago."

"A private collector, eh? I know several who'd pay handsomely for this. How much is it worth?"

She shrugged. "Artistically and historically, it's very valuable and rare. But I have no idea what provenance it has or even if the Japanese government may try to claim it under antiquity export regulations."

"Yes, yes." He waved impatiently. "And monetarily?"

"Nigel, I haven't discussed any of this with the book's owner."

"As a favor to me, your boss."

She narrowed her eyes. Nigel claimed discussing money was crass. At least that's what he told her when she tried to get a raise last spring. Still, she did report to him. Lucky her. "Possibly forty or fifty thousand dollars, maybe more at an auction with significant interest."

"Indeed." He steepled his thin, white fingers and rested his receding chin on them. "So the current owner wants to sell the collection?"

Meg realized she had no idea what Rick's plans were. "I don't think he's decided."

Nigel leaned over and caught her cotton-gloved hand in his. "Perhaps you could *help* him decide."

Ugh, he was holding her hand? Nigel never touched

anybody, and Meg had always thought he was pretty much asexual. At least the glove kept her skin from touching his. She tried to tug free. He hung on tight, so she pressed her acrylic-covered thumbnail against the pressure point between his thumb and forefinger like Uncle Yoshi had taught her in their judo lessons. Even through the cotton, the thick plastic nail exerted plenty of force. He winced and let go, flexing his hand.

"I *have* decided." Rick had finished his cell call, his wide shoulders filling her doorway. "And it's not for sale. Not until Meg shows me everything about that book."

5

THE TWEEDY DWEEB badgering Meg changed his tune immediately, his haughty look whisked away by an ingratiating expression. "So you're saying you might consider selling the collection if you had more information about it?"

Before Rick could answer, Meg hastily introduced them. Too bad for her, to get stuck with a boss like that. But he didn't see any harm in letting the guy twist in the wind for a while. "I need an extensive appraisal first, conducted personally by Dr. O'Malley."

"Oh, indeed, indeed." Nigel's eyes brightened. "This would be her top priority."

"Nigel," Meg interjected, "the art exhibit is my top priority this summer. We only have a few months to finish preparing it, and I'm teaching summer school as well."

"I don't see why you can't do all three. After all, my dear, an extra project like this demonstrates initiative when tenure time rolls around." Nigel turned to face Rick, fortunately missing the poisonous green daggers she shot at her boss.

Rick tried to defuse the situation. "I didn't realize Dr. O'Malley was in charge of such a large project."

That was the wrong thing to say. Meg rolled her eyes as Nigel puffed up like a skinny brown rooster. "Megan is *not* in charge. I am." He executed a neat about-face and raised his pale eyebrows at her, asserting his authority.

She gave them both a cool smile. "I'd be happy to help. I'm sure it won't take long since Mr. Sokol will be heading back to California soon."

"Actually, I'll be staying in Chicago this summer, so we'll have plenty of time to work together."

"Perfect!" Nigel's smile widened as Meg's turned speculative. "Perhaps we three can stroll over to the faculty club for a spot of tea while we discuss our mutual endeavor?"

Had he fallen into *Masterpiece Theatre?* "Sorry, old boy, the young lady has already consented to a spot of luncheon with me, and I'm sure an important scholar like you has many demands on his time."

The object of their discussion stared at him as if he'd grown two heads. She opened her mouth to argue with him, but glanced at her alternative.

"Fine, fine." Nigel was practically rubbing his hands together in anticipation of a sale as he left. "And don't be afraid to ask Megan for anything. I'm sure she'll be *most* accommodating."

Rick fought the urge to kick Nigel's skinny British bum back across the pond. Meg muttered something in Japanese that didn't sound like a compliment.

"Sorry about that." He grimaced. If he had to write a list of how to get to know Meg better, pissing off her boss and doubling her workload wouldn't be on it.

"Not your fault." Her stomach growled and she pressed it in irritation.

He checked his watch. "It's almost eleven. I'll take you to lunch."

"I wish I could, but I've got a lot of work on my plate."

"Nigel's expecting us to leave for lunch. If we're still here, he'll come back and bug us."

"I guess you're the lesser of two evils." She smiled. "But we shouldn't leave this here." She wrapped the book and slipped it carefully into his leather carry-on.

"Are you wearing those to lunch?"

"What?" She looked at her outfit.

"The white gloves. They look kind of cool with your outfit."

She stripped them off and tossed them on her desk.

Megan marched past him and flipped off the light switch. "Holly, I'm going to lunch, but I'll be back soon." She turned to leave, her sandals clicking on the linoleum.

Rick shook his head slowly behind her. Her irrepressible assistant fought back a smile. "Meg, if you want to take a long lunch, I can hold down the fort."

He nodded quickly.

Holly continued, "In fact, take the entire afternoon off. I can tell Nigel you went to the main library." Her dark eyes sparkled glancing between them. "Seven levels, two million books—he wouldn't even *try* finding you."

Rick winked and put his hand in the small of Megan's back, steering her out the door. "A pleasure to meet you, Holly."

Holly sighed behind them. "Looks like Meg will get all the pleasure."

MEG WAS STILL BLUSHING from Holly's parting comment as she and Rick stepped into the bright May sun. To mask her tumultuous feelings at seeing him again, she pulled out her white retro sunglasses and put them on. "You don't have to take me to lunch. I'm perfectly capable of managing Nigel." Although whether she was capable of matching Rick's long stride in her tight skirt and high-heeled sandals was another question.

He slowed his pace after noticing her churning legs. They probably looked like Yogi Bear and Boo Boo out for a walk. "You shouldn't let him take advantage of you. You're a tough girl. Stand up to him."

"First of all, I am not a girl. I may be short, but I am a woman."

"I did notice that."

She raised an eyebrow at his suggestive tone and forged ahead. "Second, have you ever worked in higher education?"

"Does the university cafeteria count?"

She snickered. "No. As an untenured lackey, I get

every crummy job in the department, except for those I can foist off on the grad students. So I need to keep Nigel Fitzjordan happy until that magic day when he recommends tenure for me. Then I can foist off crummy jobs onto the next untenured lackey that comes along."

"It's good to have goals." He turned into a faculty parking lot. "So what's next on your list?"

"I want to get another scholarly article accepted for publication, but it's extremely difficult to find a subject that hasn't been done to death. If I read another article on *The Tale of Genji,* I am going to scream."

"The tale of what?"

"Don't get me wrong, it's wonderful. Lady Murasaki Shikibu, a protégée of the Japanese empress, wrote it in the eleventh century and it's possibly the first novel ever written. But the academic world thrives on new and exciting research, and new and exciting research material doesn't come along often." She'd wound up writing her Ph.D. dissertation on an obscure artist from Japan's equivalent to rural Nebraska.

"New and exciting like my pillow book?"

"Ye-es." Her heels clicked slower as her brain clicked faster. "What if I wrote an article on your pillow book?"

"Mine?"

"Yes!" She grabbed his arm, barely noticing the hard bicep under her fingers. "This is perfect. No one's seen your book since the late forties. It's one of the lost wonders of Japan's *shogunate*."

He covered her hand with his. "I need my anonymity. In my line of work, I don't want my name and picture plastered all over the place."

"Sure, sure." Meg started walking again, almost skipping in excitement.

"Then I guess I'll have to think about it. Maybe you could convince me over a friendly lunch?"

Judging from the wink he sent her, he was just joking, but she fully intended to make her case. He stopped next to a gigantic silver SUV and unlocked the passenger door.

"Does this thing come with a ladder?"

"I'll give you a *friendly* boost." Grabbing her around the waist, he lifted her into the SUV.

"Is it your hand on my ass that makes it 'friendly'?"

He gave her a wide smile, showcasing his dimple. "Just helping you keep your balance, honey."

Meg was plenty off balance, even buckled securely into the monster vehicle. Rick climbed into the driver's seat and drove toward Lake Michigan, the water a brilliant azure under the cloudless sky.

"So where are we headed?" Meg unwound a bit and started to enjoy coasting along high above the ground as he turned north on Lake Shore Drive. Joggers and bicyclists weaved along the lakefront paths while small children dangled from candy-apple red monkey bars.

"I've been dying for a Chicago-style deep-dish

pizza. My favorite place in the South Loop makes it the right way. Hand-rolled yeast dough topped with about two inches of cheese and the fresh tomato sauce poured over the top."

"Sauce on top? The other deep-dish pizzas I've had are made the regular way. Sauce, then cheese."

"Cheap rip-offs. A true deep-dish takes over a half hour to bake due to the thick crust. If the cheese were on top, it'd burn."

"I enjoy a crisp, New-York style pizza myself."

His pained look rewarded her jibe. They sparred over crusts and toppings until he had parked the SUV in a downtown garage and they were seated in a dark-paneled pizza restaurant.

The waitress stopped at their table and Rick peered over his menu. "Want to share a deep-dish pizza with me?"

"You bet." She had dieted before the wedding so she didn't roll down the aisle like a green pea. But now, it was Carbo Time. And Miller Time. "Get some beer, too."

"No Bushmills?"

"Whiskey and pizza is not a good combination."

"Okay, one pitcher of beer and a large deep-dish with sausage."

Meg burst out laughing as the waitress left. *"Saah-sitch?"*

"You don't like it on your pizza?" A look of horror passed over his face. "You're not a vege-tarian, are you?"

"No, I eat meat. Were you raised here on the South Side?"

"Until I was five." He relaxed into the booth as the waitress poured their beers. "Oh, you think I have a South Side accent."

"Only for that one word."

He cleared his throat and spoke in the nasal tones of a native. "Ya wanna hear a real Sout' Side accent?"

"I'd love to. It's a welcome change from the pseudo-British tones of the university eggheads."

"When I was a kid, my family and I went over by dere to my grandmudder's house on the Sout' Side. My dad and my uncles drank Miller High Life and ate Polish saah-sitch while dey cheered for da Chicaah-go Bearsss."

She laughed and applauded. "You're quite the linguist."

He raised an eyebrow. "And I speak a few foreign languages, too."

"So, uh, which ones?" She swigged some beer, hiding her blush at her excellent recall of those oral skills.

"Aside from Sout' Side-ese, I speak Czech, some Polish and a bit of Chinese."

"No Mandarin?"

"No, only Cantonese. My company deals mostly with Hong Kong and southern China." He grimaced. "I do wish I spoke some Japanese. I've refused a couple investigations because I don't have any strong contacts there. As you know, it's a hard culture to penetrate and it's difficult to get people to open up to strangers."

"We are an inscrutable race, aren't we?"

He rolled his eyes. "You are the least inscrutable woman I've ever met. Everything you think or feel shows on your face."

"Not true!" She'd learned how to mask her emotions well as a half-foreign girl-child in a culture that valued homogeneity and masculinity. He didn't know what he was talking about.

"But when we had sex last weekend…"

Meg reached over the table and covered his mouth with her hand. "Why don't you say it a little louder, Rick? I don't think they heard you over at the university."

His cheeks widened into a grin. When his tongue traced a circle around her palm, shock waves traveled up her arm and down to her nipples. Then he found a ticklish spot and she jerked away.

He pushed the pitcher of beer to the side and leaned forward. "I could tell exactly when you were about to come because your eyes darkened to forest-green." He caught her hand and lowered his gaze to her neckline. "And your cheeks and your breasts flushed the color of a ripe peach."

The waitress delivered the heavy pizza pan with a clatter. Meg jumped and fumbled her roll of silverware, ripping the paper napkin in half before she freed her fork.

"Another beer?" he offered, as the waitress served them each a steaming piece of pizza.

She tipped up the beer mug and slowly licked the foam off her lips. "Yes, please."

He stared at her mouth, the beer forgotten.

"Rick?" She nodded at the pitcher, pleased to see him pour the amber liquor in a shaky stream.

Like boxers during a difficult match, they retreated to their opposite corners and concentrated on fueling up. Meg sliced her pizza and chewed. The stringy mozzarella cheese balanced the tangy fresh tomato sauce simmered with oregano, basil and garlic. The Italian sausage was perfectly flavored, loaded with fennel seeds, paprika and black pepper.

He made little moans as he ate his slice, obviously reveling in each bite.

"How's your *saah-sitch* taste, Rick?" She copied his Chicago accent as best as she could.

"I've never had any complaints." He grinned at her exasperated sigh. "Oh, you mean the pizza. Fine, thanks."

She quit the small talk, unable to banter and do the marvelous pizza justice at the same time. He convinced her to take another small slice and topped off her beer again.

Meg finally sat against the vinyl booth and groaned. If she breathed too deeply, she'd break her skirt's zipper. "That was delicious."

"I'm glad you enjoyed it."

She'd enjoyed spending time with him, enjoyed

it more than she should considering he was just spending the summer in Chicago. By the time she'd completed her appraisal and article, it would be the end of summer and he'd jet back to L.A. "So about the pillow book?"

"Yes, the pillow book." He drank more of his beer and stared moodily into the mug.

"You do realize the Japanese Agency for Cultural Affairs may try to claim the pillow book? They have very strict regulations about what antiquities may leave the country."

He nodded. "I realize it might fall under some antiquities law, but my grandfather came by this book legitimately. He never would have stolen it or paid pennies for it to some starving Japanese family."

Meg knew he wanted to believe that but had grown up on similar sad stories from her grandparents. She shook her head. "If I write an article on your book, they might come knocking on your door."

"Until they show up with a court order, it's private property." He spread his hands wide on the table.

Meg hurried to ease his concern. "On the other hand, finding yourself the owner of such a beautiful work of art is a rare gift."

"It helped me find you." He gave her a long, searching look that she felt all the way down to her toes, but then he turned pensive. "My grandmother is the true owner. If she knew of the book, it would upset her, and she doesn't need any more upsets since my grandfather died last summer."

"I'm sorry for your loss. Was it sudden?"

"Unfortunately, no. His prostate cancer was in remission for several years before it spread into his bones and lungs. My grandmother and the hospice nurses took care of him at home for five months, so he didn't have to die in the hospital. He was pretty much our anchor." Rick swirled his beer glass around on the slickly varnished table, drawing circles of condensation. "My grandmother's at a loss after sixty years together."

Rick seemed at a loss without his grandfather, too. "That's amazing. So many couples never even make it six months."

"And some couples shouldn't last six minutes." His mouth twisted. Did he mean the two of them? They certainly seemed compatible, at least sexually. But he smiled slightly, enough to deepen the dimple in his cheek. "My grandparents were made for each other. They dated before he joined the army. He was stationed in Tokyo for his tour of duty, and when he was discharged, they got married."

"And he never mentioned what might have happened in Tokyo?"

"My grandmother said he was calmer, more mature when he came home, but she thought it was from the pressures of army service."

It still didn't make any sense, keeping something so beautiful and rare a secret for almost sixty years. "Where on earth did it come from?"

"You're the expert, you tell me."

"Well, it's obviously from the height of the Edo period. That's eighteenth-century Tokyo, by the way. How did a collection like this wind up in Chicago?"

He shrugged. "My grandmother moved into an assisted living facility and has to sell her house. I was planning to come to Chicago for Marco's wedding and help her clean out the house. I'm glad I found it before she did."

"I'm sure," Meg agreed.

"So here we are."

Here he was, thanks to the book. Deep down, she hadn't expected to see him again and had pretty much resigned herself to thinking of him as a fond memory. Instead, her fond memory was sitting across from her, bringing with him the career equivalent of the Holy Grail.

Without thinking, she reached forward and brushed a crumb off his jaw. He caught her wrist, scraping his cheek along her palm. "What is that perfume?"

"Ylang-ylang body lotion." Her breath quickened. His lips were only millimeters from the frantic pulse of her inner wrist.

"It's different from the scent you wore Saturday."

"You're right." He remembered her perfume? "I wore a heavier jasmine blend to the wedding."

He closed his eyes and inhaled, the strong planes of his face intense with concentration. "That was spicy and sexy. This is sweeter but still sexy."

"Asian herbalists say ylang-ylang is an aphrodisiac."

His eyes flew open. "Those Asian herbalists are

right." He released her wrist and shook his head. "You did it to me again. I can't leave this booth unless the kitchen catches fire. And even then I might wait to see if the fire spreads."

An answering fire was spreading through Meg. He was offering her the summer of a lifetime, professionally, personally and sexually. She'd never met a man who'd made such an impact on all three levels. Was she ready for that? Her sensible Japanese side said, *Test the waters,* and her reckless American side said, *Dive right in.*

Rick exhaled loudly and drank his beer. "Look, let's talk about something else so I can get out of this booth. You said you were born in Japan, so how did you get a perfect American accent?"

"My father is an Irish guy from Boston who joined the navy after college. He was stationed in Japan and fell in love with my Japanese mother."

"Wow. Their families must have been surprised."

"Yeah, but they accepted the marriage. My dad's parents wanted us to come home to Boston, but my dad got a job with an American company looking to expand into Japan."

He scanned her face. "And you never ran into trouble as a green-eyed Japanese girl with an Irish name?"

She laughed, not liking the hollow note in her voice. "Of course I did. I didn't even use my name because my Japanese public school teachers couldn't pronounce 'Megan O'Malley.'"

"Not another secret identity." He groaned and shook his head, but she glimpsed the compassion in his eyes.

"Yes, for that brief time I became 'Michiko Omari,' which was as close to O'Malley as they got. After the little demons in my class reduced me to tears, my father lost his redheaded Irish temper with Japanese public education and enrolled me in the American school. My classmates were children of American diplomats and businessmen and were much more open-minded than the local yokels." She nodded at his old leather bag. "Enough about that. You need to make arrangements for that pillow book."

"It's not for sale right now, especially if that weasel boss of yours is involved." He leaned over the table. "But you're welcome to try to persuade me. By any means necessary."

Several means of persuasion flashed through Meg's mind, most of them involving several condoms and a horizontal surface. Or vertical. At this point, she wasn't picky. She mentally pinched herself to bring herself out of her reverie. "But you can't carry it around in a plastic grocery bag. It should be in a climate-controlled vault."

"I can put it in the safe at my sister's place—where I'm staying—if you'd like, but I'm not worried about anyone stealing it. Her building has tight security."

"I'm more worried about heat and humidity. Paper can be very fragile." She owed it to future scholars to care properly for the book.

"It sat in a Chicago attic for almost sixty years. I

think the air-conditioned condo will be fine for a few weeks." He reached out and played with the silk poppy in her hair. "Unless you'd like to share custody?"

"Me?" It was hard to think as he traced the curve of her ear. "I don't have a security system at my apartment."

"Then you'll have to come to my condo to study it for your scholarly article. How often do you have unlimited access to a work of art like this?" He stroked the side of her neck, looping a strand of hair around his finger. She remembered how he'd gripped her hair as he thrust into her, and closed her eyes. "Are you interested?"

Desperately so, and not only in the book. She opened her eyes. "Yes. But I'll need complete access."

"Total access. Day or night." He ran his callused finger along her upper arm. "Whenever you want it."

"Thank you." His hand covered hers, and she interlaced her small fingers with his for the first time. The touch of their palms was strangely tender, almost more intimate than their exotic sexual encounter.

"My sister's in Europe this summer. The condo has a great lake view and plenty of room." He rubbed his thumb across her knuckles. "Come over tonight."

"I'd love to. What time?" No coy response from her now that she'd made up her mind to plunge into a summer affair with Rick Sokol.

"As soon as you can." As he pulled out his PDA to input her contact info, Meg couldn't suppress a shiver of anticipation. *Jump on in, the water's fine.*

NIGEL BRAKED in front of a little hole-in-the-wall pub in a working-class suburb west of Chicago. He knew the neighborhood from his trips to the horse races but hadn't realized the pub was actually open. He'd never seen any patrons and the car park was rutted and weedy.

But an acquaintance at the racetrack had seen him trying credit card after credit card in vain for a cash advance and had suggested Nigel might want to borrow some money from a certain pub owner. On a purely informal basis, of course, and at a rather high interest rate compared to the bank, but the May Classic was fast approaching. He couldn't very well ask his banker for a loan to bet on his favorite horse, could he?

Nigel stepped out of his low-slung leased convertible and cursed as a chunk of asphalt scratched his polished cordovan loafer. He shoved open the pub's heavy wooden door. Dear God, what a dismal little cave, reeking of beer and cigarettes. He made a mental note to have his jacket and trousers dry-cleaned immediately.

The bartender glared at him, but Nigel ignored him, focusing on the small quartet of men in a large booth.

"Who the hell are you?" One man stood, his head almost touching the low ceiling.

"Nigel Fitzjordan. I am here to see Mr. Valerio regarding a private financial matter."

The oafs snickered. The large man grunted. "Alls of Mr. Valerio's matters is private. Arms out from your side."

"What?" Nigel didn't understand what he wanted

until the large man expertly frisked him. "I assure you, I have no weapon."

"Weapon, wire, whatever." He nodded at another brute of a man. "He's clean."

"Thank you." Nigel gathered his ruffled dignity and followed a pointed finger into a space that more resembled a brokerage office than a back room of a pub.

"Dr. Fitzjordan?" A young swarthy fellow stood up from his sleek steel-and-glass desk and extended his hand. "Pleased to meet you. Bobby the Nose said you might be stopping by." Behind him, a top-of-the-line laptop flashed a continuous Internet feed of race-track statistics and odds. Several postmodern paintings and sketches covered the walls. If they weren't originals, they were excellent copies.

"Mr. Valerio?" The man in the Hugo Boss clothes and Italian shoes more expensive than Nigel's did not fit his image of a private loan officer.

"Call me Gianni. I always check behind me for my father when people call me that." Gianni's affable laugh never reached his dark eyes. Nigel thought perhaps one would be wise to check behind himself often for either Mr. Valerio Senior or Junior. "So, Doctor, what can we do for you?"

Nigel launched into his prepared speech on the horse he intended to back and how he had inside in-formation contradicting the long odds posted.

Gianni listened for a minute and lifted his hand.

Nigel halted midword. "I've heard enough. How much do you want?"

"I was thinking ten thousand?"

"Ten's fine. It makes the interest calculation very easy." Gianni input some data into his laptop.

"And what is the interest rate?" Nigel hoped it wasn't much higher than his credit cards.

"Twenty percent."

"Perfect."

"Per week."

"Oh." Nigel tried to hide his shock. His first instinct was to refuse, but the race was coming up in ten days. Once he won, Gianni would have his money, Nigel would have some extra and everyone would be happy. "Fine. Where do I sign?"

"Nigel, Nigel." Again with the cold smile. "We'll shake on it like British gentlemen do. Besides, the feds can't subpoena a handshake, can they?"

Nigel shook his hand again and accepted the cash Gianni pulled out from a desk drawer. He didn't feel it wise to double-check the amount. "I shall return this as soon as possible."

Gianni escorted him out. "Don't worry, Nigel. I have a very effective collections department."

6

MEG HAD NEVER SEEN such a huge erection up close, its sleek lines jutting upward at an impossible height. She stood frozen in place, her jaw dropped in amazement.

Damned if Rick's sister's *über*-modern condo building didn't resemble a giant steel penis. Chicago's own Frank Lloyd Wright, Mies van der Rohe and Louis Sullivan would have impaled themselves on their T-squares before designing such a monstrosity.

Good thing Rick was only borrowing the condo for the summer. Otherwise, she might have second thoughts about sleeping with a man with such dubious architectural taste. She grinned. Not really. He could live in a concrete bunker and she would still jump all over him.

She let the doorman open the heavy glass doors and direct her upstairs. The rapid ride up to the sixty-third-floor condo only intensified her nervous stomach. Rick was waiting for her as she came off the elevator, his blue eyes gleaming.

"Hi, Rick." She tried to think of something sexy

and clever to say, but only managed what felt like a weak smile.

"Hello, Meg." He brushed a kiss over her cheek. His gentle touch erased her nerves and told her everything would be all right.

She turned her mouth into his, deepening the kiss until he pulled her against him. His lips were warm and firm under hers as his tongue teased the soft inside of her mouth. She bit his lower lip gently and sucked it.

He fumbled behind him for the doorknob, still holding her tightly with one arm. The door finally opened and they almost fell into the condo's foyer.

She dropped her laptop bag and purse onto the floor and shoved him against the wall. His eyes, previously hazy with lust, widened in anticipation at her aggressiveness. Now that her hands were free to play, she ran them up under his navy Polo shirt, his skin silky under her fingers. His abs were as taut as she remembered, his hard pecs a nice handful. She stopped to pinch his flat nipples into tiny peaks, smiling as he groaned and tipped his head back on the wall.

Meg pushed his shirt up and over his head. Rick eagerly stripped it off and tossed it aside. She replaced her fingers with her mouth, nibbling on the little nub nestled in crisp hair. He speared his fingers through her long, loose hair, his thumbs cradling her jaw. His cock rode hot and high in his white shorts, nudging her stomach. An answering rush of heat pulsed through her sex.

She trailed her mouth down his body, stopping at

his belly button. She darted her tongue into the indentation and he flinched. Ticklish. Good thing to know for future fun and games.

His hair thickened below his belly button and she reached for his waistband to learn how he tasted, how he'd fit into her eager mouth. She'd missed that last Saturday and fully intended to remedy that oversight.

He snapped out of his sexual fog as she tugged at his shorts. He caught her hands and she pouted. Guess she'd have to find out later.

"Oh, Meg." He was breathing hard, his face flushed even in the dim hallway. "I wanted to show you some finesse, show you I'm not a guy who pounces on a sexy woman the instant she walks through his door."

Meg slowly and deliberately licked her lips and thrust out her breasts, knowing her thin bra didn't hide evidence of her arousal. "What if I want you to pounce on me?"

She didn't have to ask twice. He caught her in his arms and practically raced through the living room. She caught a glimpse of dazzling Lake Michigan through a wall of windows, but he'd already reached the bedroom and set her on the huge bed.

Before he could pounce on her in earnest, she spotted the master bath through an open door. "Wait." She scrambled off the bed and stopped in the doorway. The room before her was almost as big as her entire apartment. Cool white tile covered the floor, matching the white plastered walls. A beautiful cobalt-blue glass sink bowl sat on top of a white distressed wood cabinet.

Her Japanese half thrilled to see a whirlpool tub big enough to do the backstroke in. Her Irish-American half was happy she didn't have to clean it.

But the bathroom's centerpiece was the magnificent shower enclosure. The tilework was a gigantic ocean wave, tiny dark blue glass tiles at the bottom fading upward into sun-dappled sea-foam green. The clear glass door didn't distract from the wonderful colors, and a clever shower seat was tiled to look like a giant oyster shell, complete with a gleaming pearl.

He had come up behind her as she examined the bath. "Maybe later we can take a nice, long shower."

The whole room was a soothing mermaid grotto, and she intended to play in it. "Rick, do you remember the pillow book painting of the woman bathing where the man watched from behind the screen?"

"Umm, yeah." She craned her neck to see his thoughtful expression turn lustful.

"Coed bathing was illegal by then, so a man wasn't allowed to share a hot bath with a woman, watch her soap up her soft slippery skin. It was a shame because men like to watch sometimes, don't they?" She moved into the bathroom and caught sight of her reflection in a large mirror mounted above an antique vanity table.

Her eyes had the same fevered glow as when she'd peered into the Palmer House elevator mirror. And now that she knew how his body could make her burn, her eyes were even brighter. She pulled open the vanity drawer for a hair clip and found a pair of decorative chopsticks. Even better. She twisted her hair up and secured it with the chopsticks.

Rick stood still behind her, buying into her pillow book fantasy. Her skin prickled with nerves and heat. A basket of brand-new bath products sat on the vanity. She picked a large sea sponge and opened the top to sniff several expensive gels and scrubs. Creamy coconut body wash fit her steamy tropical mood to a T.

Meg unbuttoned her blouse and tossed it onto a heavily padded bench. Her linen capri pants followed in quick succession, until she stood in front of the ornate gold mirror, clad only in an ivory bra and panties. The sheer fabric matched her skin tone perfectly, with only the dark circles of her nipples and shadowy pubic hair for contrast.

She wasn't the only one admiring her reflection, Rick's bold stare making her nipples pebble. He made a move toward her, but she shook her head. He stopped, his hands clenching in frustration.

Ignoring him but totally aware of him, she stripped off her underwear and sashayed into the shower. Bathing in front of a hidden lover was his fantasy, and she wanted to give it to him. He sat on the padded vanity seat, his large frame even more masculine contrasted against the cream velvet cushion.

She needed a few seconds to figure out the elaborate showerhead system but finally twisted the right handles, setting off a deluge of water. She didn't turn on the separate shower on the opposite wall, having no desire to reenact the flooded compartment scene from *Titanic*.

She squealed as hidden jets sprayed her already sensitive nipples. A third jet of water hit her in the ass, making her jump.

Rick let out a guffaw louder than the rushing water. So he thought that was funny? They'd see who was laughing after she got through with him.

After adjusting the water pressure, she poured a ribbon of body wash onto the sea sponge and squeezed the suds throughout. The heavy, sweet scent of coconut reminded her of hot days lying on the beach, where her body was so relaxed she almost melted into the sand. The last time she'd had that bone-deep relaxation was after having sex with Rick.

A shiver of anticipation ran down her spine despite the warm water. She ran the sponge across her arms and throat, sighing softly as the city dust and sweat melted away. Lifting her elbow, she lathered the nape of her neck, making sure her breasts were thrust out in profile.

The plan was working, she found, as she sneaked a sideways look at her target. Rick stared hungrily at her. Remembering how he loved playing with her breasts, she held the sponge to the hollow of her throat and squeezed sudsy rivulets over each breast. The soap bubbles caught on the tips, dripping off in slow plops onto the midnight-blue tile below.

Meg massaged the coconut wash into her breasts. Mmm. Her nipples slid between slick fingers. She slowed her pace and pinched her nipples gently, pulling at them until they were agonizingly tight. Aside from perfunctory self-exams, she'd never taken the time to explore her breasts before. They were small, she had to admit, but amazingly sensitive. And with Rick watching every touch and caress, they were responding like never before, sending waves of pleasure from her belly to the throbbing wetness between her legs.

She brushed the sponge across her nipples, the natural material's crevices and nubbins rippling across the taut peaks. She closed her eyes and imagined his rough tongue lapping at her engorged flesh.

Her legs wobbled underneath her, so she sat on the oyster shell seat. She flinched at the cold grayish-white tiles, but her superheated body quickly warmed them.

Even through the water-spotted glass, she saw the tension radiating off Rick. His fingers dug into the cushion as if he were clutching at his self-control. His erection straining against the front of his white shorts reminded her of a besieged warrior waving a samurai sword in defiance.

She planned to push him to the brink of total surrender. She spread her knees, knowing she was giving him a good view of her pink inner flesh.

Starting at her left ankle, she smoothed the sponge to the crease where her thigh met her hip. She soaped her belly button, letting the foam drip into the black hair below. Purposely skipping her moist center, she leaned forward to run the sponge down her right leg. Her slick breasts rubbed across her thighs.

Squeezing more coconut wash on the sponge, she finally brought it to the swollen folds between her legs. The nubbins scraped and slipped over her clit, rough, then smooth. She pinched her nipple as she massaged the sponge in tiny circles.

For the past week she had been unbearably aroused. She didn't know how long she'd be with Rick, but once he was gone, she'd at least have some memories for those late nights.

Rick's gaze, bluer than the expensive glass tile, locked with hers. He stood, knocking the seat over with a crash as he toed off his shoes and tossed his gold watch on the vanity top. "Meg!" His voice was hungry, urgent.

She shook her head. He clenched his fists and shoved them into his pockets.

The memory of his touch intensified the throbbing between her legs. The pressure from the sponge wasn't enough any more. Meg slid it to her aching passage, making sure to lather well.

Rick was going crazy. She smiled and tipped her head against the wall. Tossing the sponge aside, Meg pushed two fingers inside herself, her inner muscles eagerly clasping them. No wonder guys went nuts for sex. Her fingers were having fun, and they were nowhere near as sensitive as a man's cock.

Rick's hand was busy, too. He started to adjust his erection and shoved his shorts off instead. His cock stood out proudly from his belly, dark red and glistening with desire.

In and out, she massaged her clit with her other hand. Rick copied her actions, wrapping his left hand around his cock to relieve some pent-up desire. He was indeed a lefty, judging from his long, strong strokes.

The ultimate pillow book voyeur fantasy. The sight of her bathing was driving him so close to the edge that he had to touch himself.

She slowed her caresses, easing herself down from the peak she'd approached. It was time for Michiko to come out and play.

Recoiling in mock shock, she cracked open the shower door. "Sir, you should not be here. The new rules forbid a man and a woman from bathing together." She dropped her gaze shyly, peeking at his heavily muscled chest. A thick mat of reddish-brown hair narrowed into an arrow pointing South. His coppery nipples were tight and dark.

He stalked toward her, his erection bobbing with every step. But judging from his iron self-control until now, she didn't think he planned to make it easy for her. This man was a challenge who would never bore her.

"I don't need a bath. I'm looking for something else that's wet." Rick stepped inside the shower, tossing a condom packet on the soap dish. Jets of water dampened his auburn hair, which he flipped out of his eyes with one hand. Silver rivulets traced the solid muscles of his chest, puddled in his belly button, and disappeared into the thick hair surrounding his erection.

"Do the new rules forbid this?" He captured her mouth with his, his tongue diving deep between her lips. Meg stood on tiptoe and pressed her slick body against his. Her nipples caught on his belly like they had on the sponge, his body heat warming her cool skin. She stepped on the sponge and he caught her around the waist before she fell. "Right where I want you."

"I can tell." She arched an eyebrow and closed her hand around his cock. "Or is this right where you want me?"

He shuddered as she stroked his long, hot length, enfolding her in his arms. "Oh, yeah."

Her hair slid free of the chopsticks, and she tossed them over the shower door.

"Thank God." He lifted his head from where he'd been nuzzling her neck and smiled. "I almost lost an eye."

She increased the speed of her caresses. "You don't want to wear a pirate's eye patch?"

"I love to sail, but that's taking it a bit far." He gently disengaged her fingers. "Time for you to get wet." He spun her away from him. His cock pressed into her spine, sparking an answering throb between her thighs.

"Look at yourself." Rick's voice echoed over the rushing water as he smoothed away the last traces of soap.

Meg looked her fill. He cupped her breasts gently in his big hands so the jets of hot water stung her with pinpoint accuracy. Her pale, soft flesh contrasted with his sun-darkened, callused hands. "Rick, I don't know...."

"Does it hurt?" He twisted a dial.

"That's better." She leaned against his chest. Now a different spigot poured a warm waterfall over their bodies. It was as if they stood in a tropical oasis, a hidden paradise only for two.

"You have the most amazing coral-pink nipples. I barely touch them and you go wild." He thumbed one and she shivered. "Even your heart thunders when it's against my cheek."

He ground his hips against her, his erection tracing a hot trail up her back, his balls rubbing her ass. "This is all *because* of you, all *for* you."

She didn't have time to demur before he pulled her onto his lap.

He flinched as his butt touched the shower seat. "Damn, this tile is cold!"

Meg tossed her wet hair out of her face and laughed until she gasped for air.

"You think that's funny?" He settled her more securely in the vee of his legs, running his hands up and down her sides.

"Yeah, I do." She nuzzled her cheek into his chest. Since his nipple was so close-to-hand, or rather, close-to-mouth, she leaned over and sucked it deep, rasping it with her teeth until he moaned, slipping his fingers over her ass.

"Is my nipple still attached?" He made a big show of checking his chest for bruises, but his erection flexed higher as he explored his own taut peak.

"Oh, yeah." She gave him a cheeky grin, remembering how he'd gone crazy when she bit him.

"I think you could use a tickling, young lady." He twisted a shower valve.

"What are you going to do, tickle me with water?"

"Exactly."

She laughed until a spray of water hit her in the knees. His big hands pulled her thighs apart and the water wasn't hitting her knees anymore.

A jet of water streamed over her inner sex. She wiggled in his grasp, but he nuzzled her neck. "Pretend you're in the ocean." His hot mouth slipped along her skin.

She took a deep breath and relaxed against his chest. "Okay."

"Little waves washing over the seashell, coaxing it open." He opened her fully with two long fingers. "And look, a slippery little pearl."

He touched her and she gasped. Already sensitized by the sponge massage, her clit swelled under his tiny circular pattern. Warm water sluiced into her throbbing vagina, tantalizing her but never filling her.

She rotated her hips into his drugging touch, desperate for release from the watery caresses of a thousand fingers. "I can't take much more."

He grunted and stood, his cock rubbing between her legs. Hot hands grabbed her ass and turned her to face him. He sheathed himself with one hand and steadied her when she slipped on some suds. "You don't look like you have your sea legs yet."

"My legs are fine, sailor." Throwing her arms around his neck, Meg hiked her legs around his waist.

He pressed her against the slick tile, his hands cupping her buttocks, his cock prodding her innermost folds. He glided inside, her tiny muscles loving every inch of him.

Meg locked him in place with her strong calves. Her fingers dug into his shoulders. "More." He grunted in response and sped his thrusts. She lifted her hips to match his rhythm.

He buried his face in the crook of her neck, his mouth open and gasping. "Please, please tell me you're close."

"Here." She tugged his wrist away from her butt and brought his hand around to where their bodies joined.

He got the message and flicked her clit. "There?"

"Oh, yeah." His penis thrust to the hilt as he easily balanced both their bodies, his strong buttocks flexing under her calves. Meg swelled around him and shuddered.

Rick gave her another dimpled grin. "You like it hot and wet, don't you?"

His chest was warm against her breasts and belly, the tiled wall cool against her back. She couldn't reply, focused only on the sensual maelstrom that swirled between her thighs to spread through her entire body. But his cock and fingers were hot inside her and on her, tumbling her into a wild whirlpool of sensual exhilaration. As she was about to drown in the deluge of sensations, his mouth fastened over hers and brought her safely to shore, anchoring her breath to his.

He slowed his pace, allowing her to catch her breath as she clung to him.

"Wow." She rested her head on his slick chest.

"Wow is right." He shifted their bodies slightly, reaching around her to grab her ass again.

"Are you doing that to keep your balance or because you like my butt?" she asked, smiling.

"Both. I'm an expert at multitasking." He kissed her tenderly.

"Can you add a third thing to your job list?"

"What?"

"I want you to thrust hard and fast until you come."

"Done and done." He lived up to his promise and immediately lost himself in deep, long strokes. His dimple disappeared as his face drew into taut lines, his eyes crinkled as if in pain.

She rested her foot on the shower seat as his hard thrusts threatened to unbalance them. He didn't lose a beat, filling her over and over again as the steam curled to the ceiling. Her fingers played with the wet curls at his neck until he gritted his teeth and drove into her.

"Oh, baby…" His sentence trailed off into a wordless groan. He twisted his hips, his cock jerking and pulsing inside her in a broken rhythm.

She grabbed his shoulders as he staggered a bit. "Careful."

"Right." He turned and sat on the seat, sending shivers through her body where they were still joined. "I'd hate to explain to the paramedics how we both broke our hips in the shower."

"This is quite the bathroom." She straddled his lap. "I feel like a mermaid."

"You're more like a sea siren, luring me into your clutches."

Meg used her internal muscles to squeeze his still-impressive erection. "And what do you think of my clutches?"

He shuddered in aftershock. "I don't want to escape them." Pulling her against his chest, he rested his chin on the top of her head.

Meg listened to his slowing heartbeat and tried to calm her own racing thoughts. Rick was the summer fling she'd never had as a teenager. He was the totally hot boy stuck visiting Grandma for the summer, and she was the convenient plain-Jane girl next door. In the fall he'd return to California and she'd start school, sadder and wiser.

She smiled at the gorgeous man slumping against her, his eyes closed in sexual exhaustion. Her life was like a teen novel, only with hot grown-up sex. Who said that was a bad thing?

THE NEXT MORNING, Meg awoke alone in the large bed, its heavy walnut posts stretching almost to the ceiling. She sat up and tucked the fine white sheet around her bare breasts. A white bathrobe lay across the foot of the bed with a single pink rose placed on top.

Meg picked up the rose, a goofy grin crossing her face. She sniffed at the bud as she slipped into the robe to look for Rick.

After the hallway's relative dimness, the living room exploded like a sunburst.

"What a place!" Cerulean Lake Michigan glittered through a wall of glass across the room. She walked closer, passing white nubby couches set in a wide U-shape with cobalt-blue throw pillows. Tiny sailboats dotted the water like buoy markers.

"Glad you like it." Rick came out of what she assumed was the kitchen, carrying a platter with Danishes and two glasses of orange juice. He wore a matching bathrobe, his tousled hair glinting red in the morning sunlight.

The condo was decorated like a Grecian villa, its white textured walls splashed with colorful artwork. The dining room angled off into an L-shape, loaded with a rustic dark wooden table and heavy chairs. The design was deceptively simple but obviously pricey. "It's like we're overlooking the Aegean Sea."

"My younger sister Cara decorated it for her husband, Constantine." He sighed, setting the food on the dining table. "Con loved living here, said it reminded him of home. Unfortunately, he died recently of a heart attack."

"How awful to be widowed so young." She pulled out a chair, startled when he held it for her as she sat. Geez, who had she been hanging out with that even basic table manners were a pleasant surprise? Oh yeah, her students and her ex.

"Yeah, my sister took his death pretty badly. Con was only in his late thirties." He shook his head and sat across from her. "Considering how my parents acted when we were growing up, I was amazed she even got married. The whole marriage thing is such a gamble."

Warning received, loud and clear. She supposed there had been more than one chickie who doodled "Mrs. Radek Sokol" in her notebook, but not Meg. Right now, she was more likely to doodle "Do me."

She grinned at him as he sipped his OJ. "I think about marriage often."

He choked for a second on the juice. "You do?" The panicked look on his face was priceless.

"Every time I delete my mother's e-mails. She usually attaches photos of men she'd like me to meet." Meg took a big bite of Danish. Yum, cherry. Her favorite.

"Oh." His shoulders relaxed as he reached for another pastry. "Have you gone out with any of them?"

"Nope. I'm too busy to fly to Japan for blind dates."

"Japan's loss is my gain." Before she could reply to his intriguing statement, he said, "Eat up. I know you're dying to see more of that pillow book. I look forward to learning all about it."

Meg looked forward to teaching him. Not that he needed any pointers in the sex department. If he got any better, she'd probably lose her voice from all the moaning and screaming he'd elicit from her. Speaking of, her voice *was* a little hoarse this morning.

She reached for her juice. "What, no *grappa* or *ouzo?*" Jackie O and Ari would have felt at home in the luxurious condo.

He grinned. "No, and you can't throw your glass into the fireplace, either."

"I guess I'll have to control my destructive tendencies and look at the pillow book instead." Meg finished her breakfast and washed the crumbs from her hands at one of the kitchen sinks. Her cotton gloves were still in the laptop bag, which she rescued from the foyer floor.

"And here it is." He had pulled out the pillow book and set it on a glass coffee table in front of the sofa.

"Many pillow books were wedding gifts to help the newlyweds in their marital relationship." She flipped the book open with her gloved hands.

Rick's russet eyebrows climbed his forehead and he whistled. "Talk about starting off with a bang."

A lovely woman leaned on her elbows and rested her long black tresses on the woven *tatami* mat. Her white hands stroked her lover's huge erection as he leaned sideways, inserting two fingers into her vulva.

Meg couldn't help flicking a glance at Rick's crotch. Unfortunately, he caught her and boomed out a laugh. "Sorry if I don't, uh, measure up to these paintings."

A flush crawled up her neck but she decided to bluff it out. "The exaggerated erection is an expected artistic convention of the entire *shunga* genre." She gave him a haughty stare, spoiled by the giggle she couldn't suppress.

"Kind of like huge breasts in American men's magazines." The skin around his eyes crinkled when he grinned. "Maybe you should write a scholarly paper comparing the two."

"These paintings," she said, tapping the book with a gloved finger, "have lasted for over two hundred years because of their beauty and worth. In two hundred years, those glossy, stapled centerfolds will be wasting space in a landfill somewhere."

"Okay, okay." He raised his hands in mock surrender. "But I still don't understand the genre's conventions, as you put it. That couple doesn't even look like they're having fun."

She frowned at the painting. That position sure looked fun to her. Maybe something to try out later. "Of course they're having fun."

He shrugged. "How can you tell? Their expressions are the same, whether they're drinking tea or having anatomically impossible sex."

"Oh, I understand. Don't look at their faces."

He moved close enough that his nose nuzzled her cheek. "But I think a woman's face is the sexiest part of her body when she makes love." He planted little kisses across her ear. "How she bites her pouty lower lip and lets out a little moan." He nipped Meg's bottom lip and she did moan, much to her shock.

He continued as she swayed into him, her robe opening. "How her cheeks flush, how her eyes squeeze shut when she's ready to come."

Meg's eyes closed, remembering climaxing in his arms three or four times last night. She felt his weight shift as he slid behind her on the couch. His long legs rested around hers and he pulled her back into his chest. "Tell me more, honey."

She flipped the page with a shaky hand. The man in the picture had his hand inside the woman's kimono, obviously fondling her breast. The kimono gaped open, baring the woman's pink sex. "This is—" She gasped as Rick cupped her breast, brushing his thumb lazily over her nipple.

"What?" he said innocently, slowly pulling the bottom half of her robe to the side to uncover her thigh. Soon Meg matched the picture. She turned in his arms and grabbed at his head to kiss him.

"No, no, honey. You want to keep your gloves clean." He detached her hands and faced her away from him.

So he wanted to tease her. She was more than willing and wiggled back into the vee of his legs. The hardness pressing into her back wasn't his bathrobe belt knot.

"You can often tell the time period by the clothes they're wearing—"

"Or not wearing," he interjected, one hand strumming her nipple. His other hand rested briefly on her knee and slid up her thigh. She tensed in anticipation as his fingers brushed the seam of her sex.

She let out a groan as he spread her gently, his long finger homing in on her clit. He circled the tiny nub with a lazy touch. "Go on, sweetheart. I love hearing you dive deep into your subject." He slipped his finger deep into her vagina at the same time he pinched her nipple.

She spasmed around his finger, her head lolling

back on his shoulder. He added another finger and thumbed her clit. She thrust her hips into his hand. His cock had escaped his bathrobe, its hot length pressing her back. Just as he was about to bring her to a blazing climax, he slowed his pace.

"No!" She tried to twist free to climb on top of him and finish the job, but he pinned her to his hard body.

"I'm sorry, did you want me to stop?" He withdrew a finger and she whimpered, shaking from her thwarted orgasm. "Turn the page now."

"You sure do like this pillow book," she blustered, complying anyway.

"I sure like *you*. The first time I looked at the book, all I thought of was you, your long dark hair sliding over me as we tried out two or three or ten poses." He licked the outer curve of her ear. "I got a hard-on right there, and I came in the shower that night calling your name."

"Calling for Michiko?" It was a silly point to make considering the man had his finger resting somewhere in the vicinity of her G-spot, but Meg couldn't leave it alone.

"Calling for *you*. 'A rose by any other name would smell as sweet.'" He kissed her neck.

A man who could quote Shakespeare's *Romeo and Juliet* in the middle of hot, sweaty sex was a keeper. But only for the summer.

Meg focused her unseeing eyes on the painting in front of her. A young woman in an elaborate kimono strolled under a flowering cherry tree. She pointed to the flowing script inked above the pastcl-clad figure. "This is a poem in haiku form. 'I am a fragrant cherry blossom/Petals wet with dew/Falling into his cupped hands.'"

He stared at the gracefully inked lines. "That poem is pretty, but what does it mean?" He knew damn well what the haiku meant. She could tell that from how his muscular chest rose and fell more rapidly.

"I'm sure you can figure it out." The image of her damp pink petals falling into Rick's hands brought a fresh surge of dew between her thighs.

"'You are a fragrant cherry blossom.'" He circled her clit with the fresh moisture, inserting a second finger again. "Your soft pink petals wet with dew, falling into my hands."

She tipped her head to the side, her breath coming faster as he sped up his caresses. Her gloved hands clenched into fists on his knees. "More." She thrashed her head back and forth, her hair rasping over his bare chest.

"So wet and soft." He spread his big hand over her breasts, teasing both nipples at once. Meg strained into his touch. Her thighs started to shake from the building tension. He nuzzled her neck, nipping her earlobe between his teeth. Then one finger found a sensitive bud deep inside her and pressed hard.

Meg's orgasm bloomed out from his finger, rippling in waves through her pelvis up to her breasts. "Oh, Rick—" His name trailed off into a wordless cry.

"Yeah, that's it, baby." His hands were relentless, plucking at her until she was gasping for air.

She collapsed on his chest, her heart pounding. He finally withdrew his fingers. Instead of wiping them on his robe, he deliberately brought them to his mouth and sucked them clean before her shocked stare. "Sweet cherry nectar."

Meg started to get aroused all over again and grabbed his lapels. "Take me to bed right now."

He laughed and swung her into his arms. "Good. I want to recreate that first painting. My appreciation for dirty Japanese pictures grows every day."

She groaned and bit his neck in mock punishment. "I'll make an art lover out of you yet."

"That comes second. Being *your* lover comes first," he promised.

7

EVEN THE STACK of work on Meg's desk couldn't dampen her mood. She'd had a permanent grin on her face in the three weeks since they'd first made love at the condo. Her apartment near campus had seen several risqué encounters as well, although he complained that her futon had half crippled him. That was definitely his only complaint about staying in her bed.

Her cell phone chirped on the desk. The caller ID showed Rey's number, so she eagerly answered. "Rey! How was the honeymoon?"

"Wonderful! We had so much fun on that cruise. It was so sweet of Marco to plan a trip around the Mediterranean for us. He knows how much I love Italy and the south of France."

"And how much of Italy and the south of France did you actually see?"

Her friend laughed. "We were a bit late for shore excursions but did manage to see more than the inside of our suite."

"I got your postcard of Botticelli's Venus with

Rick Sokol's cell phone number on it." The print of a naked Venus on a clamshell was tucked into her dresser mirror's frame and never failed to remind her of Rick's wonderful shower.

"And I've been dying to know what on earth happened during our reception, especially when you showed up looking like something the cat dragged in, and he showed up looking for a green-eyed Japanese girl named Michiko."

"More like the cat that swallowed the canary. I decided to get in touch with my Japanese side." Meg explained her little deception and hinted vaguely at her upstairs activities.

"Well, whatever you got in touch with sure got in touch with him. You did call him, didn't you? I know you're busy with summer school and the art exhibition...."

"I'm busy, not crazy, but I didn't have to call him. He found me at the university the Monday after your wedding." She rubbed her ear at Rey's excited squeal. "Take it easy. He brought a book of *shunga* for me to appraise. Otherwise, who knows if he would have bothered? I haven't exactly hung up my bridal kimono in my living room to moon over it."

"Give me a break." Meg could practically see Rey putting her hands on her hips. "You should have seen the disappointed look on his face when he realized you'd gone. And he is such a nice guy, especially after that worthless, no-good Ethan."

"Rey!" Meg forced herself to take a deep breath.

Her stomach still knotted up if she dwelled too much on that terminated relationship. "I can tell Rick's not like my sleazy ex, but beyond that, we're still getting to know each other."

"Make sure he gets to know all of you. You pulled him in with your sweet Japanese side so keep him hooked with your wild Southern California side."

Meg frowned. Just because she occasionally— okay, frequently—swore and could hold more liquor than a typical woman her size didn't mean she had no tender side. "I *am* sweet."

"I know you are, but almost no one else does. You need to let somebody in, get close to someone." Rey pronounced her pop-psych prescription with all the solemnity of an Oprah guest.

She couldn't help but snigger. "Let somebody in? I think I've managed that frequently in the past few weeks."

"Meg!" Rey tried to sound serious but broke into laughter. "Sex, sex, sex. Is that all you think about?"

"Says a woman whose most scenic honeymoon view was the bedroom ceiling."

"All right, no more lectures, although I am quite pleased with myself. I thought you and Rick might hit it off after Marco told me Rick's last couple of girlfriends were Asian, too."

"They were?" Meg blinked a couple times. They hadn't broached the subject of previous relationships except to say when they'd ended and how long they'd been together.

"Sure. You know he's been traveling to China and Hong Kong quite a bit."

"Oh." If he liked dating Asian girls, what better place than Hong Kong? Meeting her in Chicago must have been like finding sweet-bean paste in a teacake, a pleasant surprise.

But no. She couldn't go through life being suspicious and wary, especially when Rick hadn't done anything to warrant it. Her stomach loosened and she paid attention to what Rey was saying.

"And what's this about a book of *shunga?* Marco didn't mention Rick was an Asian art collector, otherwise I definitely would have set you up with him."

Meg laughed. "An unwitting collector. He came into the artwork unexpectedly and had no idea what it was. It's absolutely lovely, and he's given me permission to use it for an article. The book has been privately owned for many decades and has never been studied in depth." She didn't go into any more details in order to protect Rick's privacy. He enjoyed using the book for sensual inspiration but was still reluctant to delve into his grandfather's past.

"A ground-breaking article would look fantastic on your CV. Any interest from the journals?"

"One editor wants to see it for their upcoming Asian art issue, but nothing definite." Meg looked at a pile of midterms and was glad she'd brought a sack lunch to eat while she graded. "I might not have the credentials they're looking for in their authors."

Rey scoffed. "Get real. You're the smartest woman I know. How many languages do you speak and read?"

Her cheeks heated as she leaned back in her desk chair. "Five, but I grew up speaking English and Japanese and the other three are Chinese dialects."

"So they don't count, then? Tell that to a billion Chinese." Her friend's tone firmed. "You learned all those languages and earned all those degrees. Despite what our mothers said, men do like smart women, especially smart men like Rick."

"He is smart." Meg couldn't help sighing as she remembered how his blue eyes sparkled when he laughed at one of her jokes. "And so hot. That's part of my problem. I have to keep my hands off him at least some of the time if I'm going to finish studying that book."

"Ah, I picture the two of you poring over every page together, exchanging heated glances..." Rey teased.

"As I stop midkiss to translate a practically illegible haiku," she teased back. "But you know me—I've never missed a deadline and I won't start now. My lunch is for grading midterms, my afternoon is for studying the book and my reward for a nose to the grindstone is an evening with Rick."

"That's actually part of why I was calling. I have two tickets for tonight's fund-raiser for the shelter at Asian Women's Empowerment in Uptown. I didn't realize we'd be returning the same day, and I'm too jet-lagged to go. Do you want them?"

"This isn't one of your mother's things, is it? Because that time you took me to her fund-raiser with the ancient Greek theme, she nearly disowned you and had me arrested."

"Everyone knows ancient Greek women went bare-breasted. At least we wore those gauze tube tops." Rey laughed. "And no, my mother won't be there."

"I don't know, Rey. In Uptown?" Uptown, on the North Side, was quite a hike from her South Side neighborhood.

"It's an all-you-can-eat chocolate tasting. Take Rick with. It'd do you both good to get out."

"Chocolate and Rick? How can I turn down two of my favorites?" Meg wrote down directions to the fund-raiser and made arrangements to pick up the tickets. "Thanks for the tickets. I'll bring you some chocolates if they have any extra to buy. What kind do you want?"

"Chocolate sauce. Marco loves it, too." There was a dreamy pause. "On his ice-cream cone, of course."

"Is that what they're calling it now?" That gave Meg some ideas for the rest of her date with Rick. A few strategically placed drizzles of chocolate sauce, and Rick would be one good-humored man.

"I MUST BE the luckiest man here tonight." Rick clasped her hand as they stood outside Sweet Some-things, a trendy dessert bar that was hosting the fundraiser.

"I think you're the *only* man here tonight." If he had a *yen* for Asian women, she was the stupidest woman in Chicago for bringing him. Several striking Indian women wore gorgeous embroidered saris in gold, green and blue. Some older Vietnamese ladies wore bright *ao dai,* long high-collared tunics with silk pants worn underneath, and several shapely Chinese girls wore skintight *cheongsams* slit high on the thigh.

But Rick's gaze didn't linger on anyone except her. "Did I tell you how beautiful you look?"

Meg looked down at her outfit, a pink boatneck top and ivory linen capris with elaborate embroidery at the cuffs and midheeled pink sandals. The retro look always made her channel sassy showgirl Nancy Kwan in the 1960s movie *Flower Drum Song.* "This outfit has the advantage of drawstring pants in case I eat too much chocolate."

He brushed aside her high ponytail and whispered, "You'll look even more beautiful when I pull that drawstring and you're wearing nothing but those shoes."

Meg almost grabbed his hand to drag him home to bed that minute, but they'd come to the front of the line. By the time they'd given their tickets to the pretty Indian ticket taker, Rick had written a check to the shelter and Meg had offered her interpreting and translation services one evening a week.

"You speak five languages? I'm impressed." Rick's smile turned female heads around the room. The hunkiest guy by far in the room, and he was all hers.

"Once you know one, the others are easier to learn."

"Right." He rolled his eyes. "That explains my mighty command of the Japanese language."

A blush crept up her cheeks and she fought the Japanese urge to cover her mouth and giggle self-deprecatingly. "Now let's get some chocolate."

They turned the corner into the room with the chocolate buffet. Rich, dark wood dominated, interspersed with backlit creamy *shoji*-style screens.

Meg's eyebrows shot up. "We are witnessing something intensely personal." Two sexy brunettes were feeding each other truffles. One licked a chocolate smear off her friend's finger, wrapping her tongue around to get every last bit.

"Look at that waiter." Rick nodded at a handsome young man with the well-chiseled looks of an aspiring actor. He stared glassy-eyed at the brunettes. His cheeks flushed, and he lowered his tray of empty glasses below waist level.

"Down, boy," Meg murmured. Her earlier joke to Rey about drizzling chocolate over Rick was definitely a wonderful idea.

Rick tugged her toward the buffet. "I want to get some chocolate now." He handed her an elegant glass plate in the shape of a peony.

Meg chose wafer-thin slices of flourless cake with raspberry puree, a chocolate roll cake and a lovely three-layer cake with cherry filling and shaved chocolate curls on top.

Rick spotted a booth in the corner. She took two champagne flutes off the lusty waiter's tray and sat next to Rick on the small bench, their thighs touching. "Thanks for bringing me, honey. Everything looks great. Beautiful, chocolate and a beautiful woman."

"As long as it's not one of the other women catching your eye." She stopped, horrified that she'd blurted out one of her deepest doubts. "I mean, ha ha—"

He caught her hand in his. "Meg, I'm sorry if you thought I was staring at those women eating chocolate. I was just imagining us together—"

"No." She took a deep breath. "I'm sorry for jumping to that conclusion. I didn't tell you exactly why I broke up with my last boyfriend because it was too embarrassing to admit I walked in on him, the professor, boffing one of the Asian foreign exchange students."

"Oh, Meg." His grip tightened on hers. "What a bastard. I hope you ripped him a new one."

"In two languages, no less." She tried to smile but failed miserably.

He shook his head. "Remember when we made our little bet about me finding you? I told you I wasn't a cheater. Not in bets, and not in relationships, either. My grandfather made sure to teach me how to treat a lady right."

He put his arm around her, his big body solid and warm. Meg hugged him back, her hands slipping under his navy sports coat to his fine linen shirt. "Thank you." Another hardened layer around her heart cracked and fell away like the milk chocolate on a Dove bar, leaving the mushy vanilla ice cream to melt under his warmth.

He smiled and kissed her forehead. "You mean a lot to me, Meg. I wouldn't jeopardize that."

"I care a lot for you, too." She pulled away from him and fiddled with her fork. "It's kind of tricky for me to open up to a man."

He surprised her with a hearty laugh. "No kidding. You wouldn't even tell me your full name."

"Good thing you're such a skilled investigator." Meg meant that compliment, realizing how much she would have missed if he'd never called.

"As long as you enjoy my other skills, which include feeding chocolate to gorgeous green-eyed girls named Meg." Rick's fork hovered over her plate. "Close your eyes and taste."

Meg looked into his deep blue eyes and slowly closed hers. "All right." She opened her mouth, and he fed her a forkful of the flourless cake.

"Now drink." She sipped at the flute he held to her lips, the slightly dry champagne balancing the cake's intense sweetness.

"Can I open my eyes yet?" Instead of answering, Rick gave her a mouthful of cake. Without any visual distraction, the sweet cherry juices exploded on her tongue, followed quickly by another drink of champagne.

Meg opened her eyes. "Now it's your turn." She knelt on the bench next to him, almost like a geisha conducting a tea ceremony.

She fed him bits of cake and sips of champagne until he protested, "I'm getting full, sweetheart."

A blob of frosting sat on his plate. "Give me that frosting." He picked up his fork to scrape it up and she stopped him. "With your finger."

He slowly scooped up the frosting with his long finger. She caught his wrist and guided his hand to her mouth. Delicately, she sucked him between her lips, her eyes locked with his as she swirled her tongue around the sensitive tip.

"Oh, my God." He pulled his finger free and yanked her into his arms. His mouth covered hers, the taste of chocolate and champagne on his tongue a distant second to his natural sweetness. They finally broke apart, breathing hard.

"Take me home right now." Meg hustled him out of the restaurant, only stopping to purchase two jars of gourmet chocolate sauce.

"Is one of those for me?" When she nodded, he grinned. "My second favorite topping."

"What's your favorite topping?" Maybe he was a caramel guy.

He whispered into her ear, "You."

8

MEG BENT OVER the pillow book sitting on her coffee table. Her office air-conditioning had broken, and she'd decided to work at home for the afternoon. Her stomach growled, and she checked the clock. Almost six. If Rick were around, they'd be planning dinner right now.

But he'd flown to Hong Kong yesterday after his Chinese contact had called him with a new lead in his industrial espionage case involving stolen technology. Rick was planning to pose as a businessman touring an American-owned factory to see their new manufacturing process. His secret camera would videotape a new piece of machinery patented by his client, another American manufacturer.

While he gathered evidence, Meg was gathering her own evidence about the pillow book. It appeared to be from the late 1700s and seemed to have belonged to an aristocratic lady, possibly a Lady Miyamoto. Right now Meg was deciphering the handwritten margin notes. They were written in a flowing feminine script and were mostly comments on Lord Miyamoto's sexual preferences. The note next to the woman on her hands and knees with the man thrusting into her said, "One of his favorites," and the note next to the woman pleasuring herself said "drives him into a frenzy."

She smiled. Some things never changed. But the next painting showed a man making love to a woman while a second woman peered jealously around a *shoji* screen. Lady Miyamoto had written, "My lord travels to Edo tomorrow. His former lover Lady K will be there as well. I will pleasure him deeply tonight and beg to go with him." Hmm. Lady M had some doubts about her husband's fidelity when he went out of town.

Rick had offered to take Meg to Hong Kong, but she'd fallen behind on her projects due to grading final exams and papers and couldn't afford to take off several days. Although she'd sent her man off to one of Asia's most exotic locations, she actually wasn't worried about him cheating on her. He'd promised her he wouldn't, and that was good enough for her.

Meg flipped through the book, eager to find out what had happened to Lady M. Japanese men of that era weren't concerned about being faithful to their wives, seeing it as their masculine right to have sex with as many women as they wanted.

Finally she spotted a little postscript. "My lord and I returned from our trip to Edo, spending every night together. He purchased for me a lustrous pearl necklace in remembrance of our pleasures."

Well, Meg couldn't fly off to Hong Kong for

nightly pleasures with her man, but she had one thing Lady M didn't have: a long-distance calling plan to Asia.

RICK WAS JOLTED from a restless sleep by the phone on the nightstand. 6:30 a.m. "My wakeup call was for seven," he blurted into the receiver. The phone had woken him from an erotic dream where Meg leaned over him, her dark hair swirling over his bare chest as she licked her way down his belly.

"Should I call back in a half hour?" The subject of his dream was on the other end of the line, amused at his early morning grogginess.

"Meg." He sat up in bed and ran his fingers through his messy hair, grooming himself as if she could see him. "How are you?"

"I got home from work and wanted to catch you before you left for the factory. How are you?"

"Tired. I got a late-night call that the guy who's been trying to get me some consulting jobs with L.A.-based Japanese companies just broke his leg in a car accident." Poor guy. Rick'd have his secretary send flowers and a bottle of sake. "Somewhere on the Santa Monica freeway."

"What a shame. Stupid Southern California traffic," she grumbled.

He'd forgotten how much she disliked L.A. Maybe he could change her mind. "Don't worry about that—he'll be okay, and I'll find someone else to fill in while he's recovering. Anyway, I got you a present."

"You did?" She sounded delighted.

He was glad she couldn't see the flush creeping up his neck. "Some jasmine body lotion and perfume." He'd gotten restless in his hotel room and had taken an evening stroll along Nathan Road, one of Hong Kong's busiest shopping districts. The scent of jasmine, Meg's favorite fragrance, had drawn him into an upscale lingerie boutique, where he'd stood among silk bras and panties sniffing the air like a hound dog on a trail. A lonely hound dog.

"You didn't have to do that." She was clearly pleased, though.

"I wanted to." He'd also bought her some sexy silk nightgowns, but those were a welcome home present for them both.

"Mmm. Maybe you can rub some lotion on me when you come back."

"Sounds good." It sounded better than good as he shifted in his bed, resigned to a long, cold shower after their phone conversation.

"I miss you," she whispered. "Especially at night, when you hold me close and stroke my hair."

His chest squeezed a bit at her uncharacteristically shy voice. "Me too. I love having you in my arms, your beautiful green eyes looking up at me." The word *love* came out easily, making him wonder if it had been lurking in his mind all this time. Did he love Meg? He shied away from the idea. It was much too soon, considering they lived so far apart and hadn't discussed future plans. Even if he were sure, he wouldn't say it for the first time over the phone from eight thousand miles away.

"I love being in your arms too." She paused for a second and then cleared her throat. "I know it's not nighttime, but maybe I could help you start your day off right."

"What?" His heart pounded faster.

"Get that jasmine lotion. I'll wait for you."

He cast a frantic look around his luxurious hotel room. Spotting the pink-and-white boutique bag, he leapt naked out of bed and grabbed the pale yellow bottle.

"I'm ready." He settled himself against the headboard, his palm sweating on the phone receiver.

"Are you comfortable?"

"Sure." If he considered painful arousal comfortable.

She cleared her throat. "Good. Now tuck the phone under your chin and open the lotion."

"Okay." The heady scent of jasmine filled the air, drugging his senses. It was almost as if she were in his hotel room, her perfume and husky voice tantalizing him.

"Umm, pour some into your hand and rub it across your chest."

"My chest?" He looked at the thick reddish hair there.

"Yes." Her voice was surer. "Rub it in well."

He complied, flinching slightly at the cold sensation. "I can't go to my meeting smelling like jasmine."

"So take a shower after we get off the phone." She laughed. "If you do what I say, you won't need cold water."

"Hot damn. Now what?"

"Take your slick hand and pinch your nipple."

"Meg…" He wanted to get to the main event, his penis straining toward his belly.

"Pretend it's my wet mouth nibbling on you."

Rick moved his hand over to one flat nipple, closing his eyes and imagining her in front of him. He pinched himself tentatively, and then harder. He moaned into the receiver as a jolt of lust shot from his nipple to his cock.

"What are you thinking of?" Her voice was low and silky smooth.

"How you bit me the first time we made love."

"And you liked it, didn't you?" Without waiting for an answer, she continued, "Now the other one."

He had never realized how sensitive his nipples were. Reluctant to stop pinching himself, he dropped the lotion bottle on the bed and used both hands, his nipples tight and hard. His pelvis thrust convulsively into empty air. "More, Meg, I need more."

"Get more lotion and rub your belly. Nothing below the waist."

"God, you are a tough one." His slippery hands were already fumbling the bottle open.

"Just call me Mistress Meg."

He groaned, the image of her in black leathers and stiletto heels filling his brain as his fingers tangled in the dense hair below his navel. "I did what you asked." He was shocked to hear how needy he sounded.

"Good." Her breathing was coming faster, too. "Since you obeyed my commands, you may wrap one hand around your hard cock."

His only reply was a wordless groan. He thrust into his slippery palm, pretending Meg was enfolding him in her tight, wet warmth. "Feels good." He dug his heels into the bed as his body arched off the mattress.

She laughed. "Slow down, slow down. I have plenty of long-distance minutes."

He forced himself to ease up, wanting their game to continue. Sweat trickled into the lotion. "What next?"

Her phone clicked. "My call waiting is going off, do you mind if I put you on hold?"

His bellow of protest mixed with her uproarious giggles.

"Rick, I'm joking." She stopped to catch her breath. "Oh, if only I could have seen the expression on your face."

"Ha, ha." He smiled ruefully, regaining some self-control. "If you don't help me here, the top of my head may explode and I won't be fit for any more business trips."

"Good. I'll keep you all to myself, and your only job will be to satisfy my every desire."

He groaned, images of black leather and his four-poster bed filling his mind.

"Where were we?" she teased.

"I was wrapping my hand around my cock and you were talking dirty to me."

"Oh, that's right. I was going to have you slide your hand to the tip of your cock and swirl your palm around."

He obeyed and panted, his juices dribbling out.

"Now stroke down."

Every cord and vein on his penis bulged as he cupped himself and pulled with long, strong strokes.

"Are you close, lover?"

He nodded, causing the phone to slip. Jamming it under his jaw, he gasped some kind of affirmative.

"You'll need both hands for this, so set the phone next to your head so you can hear me. And so I can hear you when you come."

Easing flat on the mattress, he bent his legs and arranged the receiver as she asked. "I can't take much more, sweetheart."

"You've been very obedient, so now you get your reward. Remember when I cupped your balls? Do that again while your slick hand moves up and down on your shaft."

"Ohhh…" His testicles were pulled tight against his body, eager to spill forth as he gently rolled them in his palm. He pushed his penis into his other hand, the dizzying aroma of jasmine surrounding him, almost as if he was plunging deep into Meg's welcoming body.

Her sultry voice whispered encouragement into his ear, telling him how much she loved touching his cock and how sexy she felt when he came inside her.

He gritted his teeth and exploded, his seed rock-eting on to his belly in several long spurts. His breath rasped into the silent hotel room, gradually quieting.

"Rick? Are you okay?"

"Still recovering from one hell of a wakeup call."

"Glad to help you start your day with a bang." She laughed.

"And what about your long, lonely night without me, Meg? Can I satisfy you tonight?"

"How?" Her voice got breathier.

"Tell me what you're wearing."

Oh, wow. Meg shifted on her couch and looked down at her outfit. She hadn't changed yet from her work clothes. "My orange top and matching poppy skirt. With those high-heeled sandals and no stockings. It's eighty-five degrees here."

"What about underwear, honey? You're not being naughty and going commando again, are you?" Rick had teased her about leaving her panties in the Palmer House bedroom as a clue for him to follow.

"Thong panties. No bra today." She didn't always need one and it was just too hot.

"And I bet you liked your bare breasts rubbing against that soft fabric. Touch your little nipples to feel how hard they can get."

Meg complied, her breasts instantly tightening. The friction had been arousing her all day, when she couldn't do anything about it. Now she could, teasing and pulling at them until she squirmed on the couch.

"Was that a moan, Mistress Meg? Do you need more than that?"

She gasped a "yes" and waited for his next instruction.

His voice deepened. "Put your hand on your ankle and slide it all the way up your bare leg, right to that place I love to touch."

She looked down at her knees and slowly let them fall apart as she touched her ankle and did what he asked, closing her eyes to pretend he was with her. Her skin was smooth and freshly shaved, her judo-hardened muscles firm and resilient. She imagined them wrapped around Rick's waist. A burst of fresh moisture dampened her fingers through the thin thong. "My hand's there."

"Where, honey? Your pussy?"

"Rick!" Her face flamed.

He laughed. "So tough on the outside, but you blush at one naughty little word."

"How did you know I'm blushing?" she demanded.

His voice was low and intimate. "Because I know my Megan Michiko O'Malley, that's how."

"Oh, Rick." She swallowed a lump in her throat. "You're so sweet."

"Not as sweet as you are, baby. And not as sweet as that naughty place that shall remain nameless."

She burst out laughing until he said, "The place where I'm dying to be. Pull aside your thong, just like I do when I'm entering you. Pretend I'm so hot for you, I can't wait for you to undress."

Meg slid her fingers between her wet folds and spread the moisture up to her clit. Her head fell back on the couch as the little nub hardened under her eager touch. His voice provided the soundtrack for the erotic film playing in her mind. "Now I'm touching you nice and slow, then faster until your breath comes fast and you want to come even faster."

She groaned his name and braced her shaking heels on the coffee table to get better leverage as she sped up her caresses. Lust twisted tight in her belly, radiating up to her nipples where they jutted against her sweater.

"Remember when we looked at the pillow book together and I slid my fingers inside? Do that, and pretend it's my cock."

Meg did as he said, using both hands to ease the burning ache. Little moans escaped into the phone receiver as she tossed her head back and forth.

"Now, Meg, come now." His forceful command snapped her control, spinning her into a climax so powerful she cried out for him. She opened her eyes as the tremors subsided, momentarily disoriented and disappointed when he wasn't there with her.

"Still there, honey?" His voice had lost its dark intensity and was back to his customary light-hearted tone.

"Yes." She sighed. "I'm still here and you're still there." Her apartment seemed unusually lonely without him. But she always had her work, didn't she?

"I should be home for the Fourth of July weekend. Can you spend it with me?"

"I'd love to. I'm not working over a holiday weekend."

"Leave it to me. I'll plan something special," he promised.

"I'll be glad to see you."

"Me too, honey." He paused for a second. "Take care."

"You, too." Meg hung up and slumped back on her couch. If she missed him this much when he was on a short business trip, what would happen when he went back to L.A.? Would they call each other at night for some naughty conversations and steal weekends here and there?

She'd have plenty of time for her career. Plenty of time to write the articles that would get her a full professorship someday. Plenty of time to sit alone on her couch and wonder if it had been worth it.

NIGEL FITZJORDAN scanned the racetrack with anticipation as the jockeys in their bright silks reined in their horses at the gate. Nigel only had eyes for one— Barry's Boy. That horse was a long shot, but Nigel's cousin's wife was the jockey's sister-in-law, and they assured him Barry's Boy was a sweet goer.

After this race, Nigel would pay off the Italian crook, pay off his credit cards and have plenty left over for a little trip to Vegas.

The starter's pistol sounded, and the horses leaped

forward. Nigel's heart was in his throat as Barry's Boy pulled in front. He silently urged the horse onward, his betting ticket crushed in his fist.

The announcer's voice was thick with excitement. "And Barry's Boy in the lead in the homestretch, with Fancy Free close behind. Barry's Boy pulling ahead, and—oh, no! Barry's Boy grabbed on the heavy track and caught his right foreleg. Is he limping? I think he is! And Fancy Free's taken the lead, with Barry's Boy dropping to last. Oh, what a race for Fancy Free!"

Nigel's arm dropped limply to his side, the betting ticket falling to the ground. Gone, all gone. The money he'd scraped off his credit cards, the money he'd borrowed from Valerio at a frightening rate of interest. All gone because that bloody clumsy horse had clipped his foreleg with his hind leg.

He turned away, unable to stomach the sight of the limping animal.

Another animal, the large hooligan belonging to Valerio, stood in his path. "Good day." Nigel tried to pass in vain.

"Not such a good day for you, professor. Sorry about da horse." The giant had the nerve to pull a sorrowful face. "And about dat other matter…" He gave a grotesque leer.

"Ah, yes. I'll be in contact with your employer in regards to that financial matter." Nigel thought frantically. He had no chance in hell of paying that thug his money.

"Da boss would like a down payment." Before Nigel could protest, the big man slipped off Nigel's gold wristwatch faster than a pickpocket. "Should be good for a coupla weeks' interest."

"I say," he protested feebly until the man glared at him.

"Da boss is a man of real refinement. He said if you was to ever find some interesting kind of art, that he would consider a portion of your debt paid."

"Art?" Nigel remembered the paintings on the mobster's wall. Not reproductions, then. "What kind of art?"

"Anything classy. And hard to trace," he quickly added.

"Classy and hard to trace." Nigel's pulse slowed a fraction. "Of course, I would waive my finder's fee."

The big man snickered. "Your finder's fee is that you *don't* find yourself in somebody's trunk."

9

MEG SCURRIED AROUND her apartment tossing sunscreen and lip balm into her beach bag. Rick was coming soon, and she was dying to see him.

He'd called her from Hong Kong the day before yesterday, his voice sending a thrill through her as he asked, "How would you like to go sailing on Lake Michigan? The weather's supposed to be beautiful this weekend. Think of it—you and me. The sun. The water. My sister's friend has a sailboat we can borrow."

"You'll have to show me what to do. I've gone out on motorboats, but not sailing."

"As long as you obey my every command, you'll be fine." His voice lowered. "You know what happens to disobedient sailors, don't you?"

"What?" Tingles of anticipation ran through her body.

"They get tied up and are completely at the captain's mercy."

She had grinned. "Or else they mutiny and tie up the captain."

"The captain might enjoy that, especially if the sailor is a scantily clad, green-eyed brunette."

Then his flight had been called and he was gone, winging his way across the Pacific. He had called again yesterday to let her know of his safe arrival but had stayed over at the condo to catch up on his sleep before their sail.

Meg stuffed her orange-and-pink beach towel on top of her sunscreen and grabbed for her ringing phone. "Hello?"

"Hi, it's me. I'm only a few blocks away. Can you meet me in front so I don't have to find a parking spot?"

"I'll be right there."

"I'm looking forward to our sail. I'll see you in a few minutes."

She said goodbye and pulled her hair into a ponytail, checking herself in the full-length closet mirror. A white-and-blue spaghetti-strap sundress covered her new swimsuit, bought especially for their sailing date.

"He better love this damn suit," she grumbled, wiggling free of yet another wedgie.

A horn sounded, so she grabbed her things and locked her apartment.

Meg clattered down the steps, bursting into the dazzling sunshine. Rick waited next to his silver SUV.

"Hey, honey." He gave her a lingering kiss on her mouth and eyeballed her. "Got your suit?"

"Yep." He'd see it for the first time on the sailboat, where she could have his undivided attention.

Another car horn interrupted them, wanting to pass on the narrow street. He boosted her into the SUV, stroking her bottom. Settling into the driver's seat, he threw it into gear and drove toward the lake.

"Which harbor are we sailing from?" Meg flipped up the visor to block the early morning sun. Rick slipped on a pair of black wraparound shades.

"Belmont Harbor, east of Wrigley Field. I stopped by the boat earlier and everything's ready."

"Wonderful." Meg was bursting with excitement and grabbed Rick's hand.

He pulled their joined hands to his mouth and kissed her knuckles. "It's been months since I've been out on the water. I'm looking forward to spending a little private time with you."

"No more urgent calls from Hong Kong?"

"No, thankfully. I think everything's ironed out, and Mr. Chen knows this is an important American holiday weekend. Short of typhoon or armed insurrection, we won't be disturbed. But I did get a couple messages from your boss."

She frowned. Nigel must have gotten Rick's cell number from Rey's honeymoon postcard she'd hung over her desk. What was Nigel doing poking around in her office? "Was he pestering you about the pillow book?"

"Yeah, I guess." He shrugged. "Ol' Nigel said something about financial arrangements to benefit both of us."

"I don't know what he's thinking. The Japanese

Agency for Cultural Affairs probably has first dibs on it if you give up ownership."

"Not gonna happen, so don't worry, sweetheart." He patted her knee with his free hand.

A white band of skin circled his right wrist. "This is the first time I haven't seen you wearing your gold watch."

"Yeah, it's an antique, so it's not waterproof. My grandfather's."

"Your grandpa Sokol's?"

He nodded, his expression hard to read behind his sunglasses. "He always let me wear it when I was a kid. After he passed away last fall, my grandmother said he wanted me to have it." Rick was quiet for a few minutes as they wove through the heavy holiday traffic. "Next time, we'll rent a cabin cruiser and head north to Milwaukee. I know a great German restaurant with all the saah-sitch you can eat."

She laughed. "What is it with you Midwestern guys and your sausages?" They stopped at a red light.

"Once you've had our saah-sitch, you're spoiled for any other." He leaned over and kissed her.

She dropped her hand on his lap. "Feels like a foot-long to me."

He barked out a laugh and moved her hand to his thigh. "Flattery will get you everywhere." He signaled and turned into the Belmont Harbor parking lot. "And we're here."

Seagulls screamed overhead as they walked toward the harbor entrance. "The boat is anchored in this slip." He stopped next to a sailboat, its crisp white hull rising and falling gently in the clean blue water.

"The boat's name is *Bobbin' Around?*"

He grinned. "The owner's name is…"

"Bob?"

"Despite the less-than-original name, it's a great boat. This is a J30 cruiser-racer. I've sailed on these in California. It's a fast boat."

"Oh, good, I love going fast."

"Me, too. A fast boat with a fast woman." She slugged him in the shoulder and he laughed. "I mean, a woman who likes going fast. See, it has a fractional rig." He pointed to what looked like a maze of ropes.

"A what?"

"The fractional rig allows you to adjust the sails effectively and reduce them when the weather turns bad. But don't worry. The nearest storm is somewhere over Iowa."

The wind whipped her ponytail away from her face, and Rick's eyes brightened. "This easterly lake wind is going to move us."

"Let's set sail and blow out of here."

"Not so fast, speedy. We'll use the engine to leave the harbor. Once we get on the open water, I'll show you how to maneuver the sails. Come into the cockpit."

She snickered.

"Geez, Meg. You have a dirty mind. Now climb in."

The cockpit was a square area leading into the sailboat's main cabin. It was set three or four feet below the boat's deck and was lined in wood slats, presumably for water to drain through. Meg planned on stretching out and sunbathing on the two matching benches lining the space. Maybe she'd even go topless.

Rick came out wearing a white life vest. "You can swim, right?"

"I don't set any speed records, but with these hips, I float well."

"Good enough. But…" He pinched her bottom and she swatted his hand. "You still need to wear a PFD, at least until you get used to the boat's movement."

"A PFD?"

"A personal flotation device." He handed her a smaller white life vest. "You can take it off when we anchor farther out for a swim."

"Okay." She started to shrug into it, examining how it zipped in the front.

Rick shook his head, a mischievous look in his eyes. "You should wear your life jacket over the least amount of clothes possible."

"Is that so?" She gave him a grin.

"You want to get the best fit possible, right?"

"Oh, of course."

"I'm afraid your sundress will have to go." Rick hooked his finger under one spaghetti strap and tugged it off her shoulder. His eyes widened as he saw the tiny red triangle barely covering her breast.

"On second thought, you could get a horrible sunburn." He pulled the strap into place, glaring at the fascinated middle-aged man in the next slip.

"No, you're right as usual." Ignoring his snort of disbelief, she shrugged the sundress off her shoulders and let it fall to the cockpit floor.

The extra sets of sit-ups at the judo *dojo* were finally worthwhile. Rick's jaw dropped, his hungry stare traveling over her tiny tomato-red string bikini. Rey had bullied her into buying it, insisting that it fit perfectly. Of course, Rey did come from Sweden, the ancestral home of clothing-optional beaches.

"What do you think?" She pirouetted slowly, his stare making her nipples tighten under the unpadded bikini cups.

"Not at all what I expected." He stepped closer and trailed his hand along the curve of her hip. "But a pleasant surprise."

"Want to help me with the vest?" She spread her arms wide and stuck out her chest.

He zipped her into it, his knuckles brushing over her nipples. "Let's hurry and get on the water where we have a bit more privacy. Otherwise, I'll drag you into the cabin and have my wicked way with you."

She laughed. "If the sailboat's a-rockin', it's not from the waves."

"All right, all right." He stroked her chin and pointed to the steps leading into the boat's interior. "Go in the cabin and pull on a pair of deck shoes. They have special traction so you won't fall overboard."

Meg found a brand-new pair of deck shoes in her size and still in the box. Rick must have burned up the phone lines from Hong Kong to have made all those arrangements in a few short days. She explored farther into the cabin, noting it was fitted out like an RV, with benches that pulled into bunks and a tiny kitchen.

"We'll be out on the water for several hours. I arranged a picnic lunch from a local boating caterer. Lobster salad, little croissants and plenty of chocolate to keep up our energy." He leered at her. "Sailing whets an appetite for many things."

"Like swimming." She sashayed past him to the cockpit. "And other things you can't do until you get out of a crowded harbor."

"I'll show you how to pilot the sailboat out of the harbor after we hoist the sails." Rick pointed out the smaller jib sail in the front and the larger mainsail in the center. "We'll use engine power, but I need to raise the sails in case the engine quits. Otherwise, we could crash into the rocks."

Meg followed him as he turned on the engine and flipped about a thousand switches. He did a great job maneuvering the boat into open water.

Finally, they were out on the lake where traffic was thin. Meg tipped her face to the sky. The wind off the lake tempered the hot July sun, but she spread some oil-free sunblock on her nose and cheeks. No sense in getting sunburned. With her freckles, she'd look like a ladybug.

She smoothed some sexy red lipgloss on and

smacked her lips. The gloss must have been stickier than she thought because she wound up spitting out a mouthful of her windblown hair. She turned her head so the ponytail stayed out of her face. "It's a beautiful day."

Rick was a wonderful sailor, moving from one task to another without missing a beat. Watching his powerful thighs flexing under his snug white shorts was another bonus.

"I'm glad you like it. The only boat I've been on for the past year has been a ferry taxi in Hong Kong."

"Where did you learn to sail?"

"My parents kept a thirty-foot sailboat at a marina in Southern California. They took my sister and me sailing at least every weekend."

"Year-round sailing. I bet you got lots of experience crewing."

"Yeah, when your father thinks he's Captain Bligh, you learn pretty quickly." His mouth twisted and he reached over to examine a rope.

"And did you ever mutiny, Mr. Christian?" Meg loved the eighties remake of *The Mutiny on the Bounty,* and Rick had the same commanding presence as Mel Gibson. She, who prided herself on her independence, found herself wanting to lean on him and take some of his strength for her own.

What would it be like to rely on a man? Not because of weakness or neediness, but because she wanted to. And could he reciprocate and rely on her? She wasn't sure. Even in their most heated moments, she sensed he was holding back some essential part of his emotions. Lost in her thoughts, she almost missed his shrug.

"I mutinied in other ways."

"How?" Rick hardly ever mentioned his parents, preferring to reminisce about his grandparents and his sister.

"Let's see. I majored in engineering at UCLA, not pre-law, which meant I couldn't take my rightful place in my father's law firm and couldn't marry his law partner's daughter. How about you?"

"Well, I left Japan right after high school to attend college at the University of Southern California. My mother was reluctant to send me overseas, but my father insisted on an American college education for his only daughter."

"UCLA's crosstown rivals."

"If you say so." She laughed. "I wasn't a sports fan. Anyway, I stayed at the university long enough to get my doctoral degree and never moved back."

"And that was rebellious?"

He had no idea. "My mother pitched a month-long hissy fit because she expected me to move back to Japan after grad school. A single Japanese girl doesn't leave home until she gets married, preferably at the youngest age legally possible. I was lucky enough to get a full-time position at Chicago University. The job market for Asian art historians stinks."

"Lucky? Why do you consider yourself lucky? Weren't your qualifications outstanding?" He leaned against the deck. "I bet you graduated with the highest honors and had your pick of jobs."

"Well, yeah, I had a couple offers on the West Coast, but I've always wanted to live in the Midwest."

He laughed. "Most people want to move to Japan or California, not the Midwest."

Meg picked at the straps on her PFD. "Not me. I never felt at home in Tokyo or L.A. I always considered the Midwest the true America, the place where moms made oddly-shaped Jell-O molds and dads ate cheeseburgers until the fat dripped from their double chins."

"Sounds like summer on the South Side. Lots of fun, aside from the stifling humidity and weird industrial smells, that is. As soon as we got old enough to fly by ourselves, my sister and I spent most of our summers here." He gazed at the lake, his thoughts far away. "My grandparents insisted. They wanted us to get a break from…"

"What?" Southern California did get pretty hot and dry during the summer, but she had the feeling he and his sister hadn't been sent to Chicago to get away from the weather.

"My parents argued. A lot." Rick pressed his lips into a thin line.

"Oh." She linked her fingers together over her knees. Sure, her parents argued from time to time, but their disagreements blew over quickly. She hadn't left Tokyo to get away from them. "That must have been rough." She clasped his hand and he gave her a half smile.

"That's part of the reason you're so much fun to spend time with, Meg. You're independent, not clingy. You have your own things going on, and you don't need me."

A couple months ago, that would have been a huge compliment. Now she wasn't sure. The wind changed as quickly as her mind, and Rick hopped up to fiddle with the sails. She stretched out on the deck chair and watched him while the sun climbed higher in the cerulean sky.

"Why are we sailing in a big circle?" She stood and rolled her shoulders under the life jacket. Her art history education had taught her to look for symbolism in practically everything she saw, and their circular journey around the lake symbolized their relationship. A fun ride, but not really going anywhere.

He looked up from where he fiddled with the big sail. *The mainsail,* she corrected herself.

"We can't sail straight into the wind, so I have to adjust the boat so we continually approach the wind at a certain angle. It's called tacking."

"Oh. Where are we going?"

"As far from anyone else as possible." He sat on the slick white fiberglass deck, dangling his long tanned legs into the cockpit. She rested her elbows on his knees, smiling as he lowered his face and kissed her.

A loud flapping noise interrupted them. He jumped to his feet. "Got some luffing going on," he called over his shoulder.

"Loving?" It was a sweet kiss, but neither had ever mentioned the L-word before outside of sexual activities, as in *I love it when you do that to me*. Anticipation curled through her stomach.

"No, L-U-F-F. *Luffing* is the sound the sail makes when it's at the wrong angle." He checked the wind and loosened a line.

"Oh. So luffing is bad and loving is good?" Meg wondered what he thought about love in general.

His face turned into the wind, so she hardly heard his quiet response. "A smart sailor knows to watch out for both."

MEG HAD SHOWN herself a surprisingly good sailor, quick and agile. He could have handled the sailboat on his own, but he had enjoyed watching her climb around on deck in her PFD and tiny bikini bottom. And speaking of bottoms, her swimsuit wasn't doing a great job of blocking the sun. "Meg, you're turning pink."

She let out a sleepy hum but didn't lift her head from the lounge chair. Late nights at work as well as late nights with him had exhausted her, so he let her sleep. He sat on the edge of her chair and squeezed a puddle of sunblock into his hands, letting his body heat and the sun warm it. The rich coconut fragrance teased his nostrils, reminding him how the coconut soapsuds had dripped off her taut nipples when they had played in the shower.

He smoothed the sunblock over her tense back

muscles. His strokes became deeper, the pressure gradually ironing out the knots.

Although it looked like her bikini ties had rubbed away some sunblock. She'd be uncomfortable for the rest of their sail if she got sunburned. Two quick tugs and the ties fell away, baring the nape of her neck and the sleek sides of her breasts. He didn't want her to get sunburned there, too, so he moved her ponytail, stroking to her hairline and curving his hands around her torso. Her body responded to his touch even in sleep, her lips parting and her curvaceous hips wiggling against the thick white beach towel.

Rick wiped his forehead, sweaty despite the cooling lake breeze.

Come to think of it, her thighs were looking a bit toasted, too. He put more sunblock in his hands and cupped her leg in his palms, smoothing upward to the soft cheeks that peeped out from her bikini bottom. To be on the safe side, he hooked a finger under the leg elastic and slipped his palm underneath.

So easy to untie the bikini bottom, free his cock from the tourniquet he called his swimsuit, and enter her with one swift stroke.

"Rick?" Meg stirred and lifted her head to gaze sleepily at him.

"Lie down, honey. I'm putting some sunblock on you." Her trusting smile made his heart flip.

"Mmm." Moaning contentedly, she snuggled into the towel.

Their boat was so far off shore that only the

highest skyscrapers were visible. No other boats were in sight. They had total privacy.

He untied her bikini bottom and peeled off the back triangle. Her ass was rounded and firm, its pale ivory color testifying to a lifetime spent under wraps. He dribbled sunblock directly on her skin, half hoping the cool lotion would wake her. Her supple flesh filled his big palms as he massaged her cheeks. His fingers splayed over her hips while his thumbs inched closer and closer to the cleft of her bottom.

She lifted her bottom toward him, the bikini falling away. He slipped his thumb between her legs to find her wet and ready.

And asleep. But not for long.

MEG WAS AWARE of Rick's touch and his intentions but at the moment she was imagining that she lay on a massage table in a beautiful Caribbean resort. Seabirds called overhead, and an ocean breeze carried away the sun's sting.

Magic hands had eased every muscle knot, cramp and strain. As if they knew she needed more, needed deep-down relaxation, the hands worked their magic on her innermost flesh, soothing and arousing her. The hands stopped. She arched in protest, and they resumed, long, hard fingers brushing against her pubic hair until she spread her thighs to grant better access. They rewarded her with deep penetration. She cried out and opened her eyes.

Rick knelt behind her on the lounge. "You like that?" His thumbs both slipped inside her again, his hands gripping her ass. She raised her head, only to drop it as his index finger made lazy circles around her clit. In and out his thumbs slid, stretching her passage.

He had aroused her to a fever pitch in her dream and continued taking her higher. She ground against his hand and gripped the deck chair's frame above her head.

His chest bumped her thigh, its heat burning hotter than the sun's rays. "If only you could see yourself, honey. Your sleek skin glistening, my hands sliding over you, inside you."

Meg hooked her toes under the chair's bottom strap, getting some leverage to thrust down on his hand. Her sensitive nipples rubbed against the soft terry cloth. He increased his pace, the chair scraping along the deck.

She squealed as he pinched her ass just enough to sting. He did it on her other cheek, and her squeal quickly turned into a moan. "Again."

"I think I owe you for that Mistress Meg phone call in my hotel room." He withdrew his thumbs and gave her a light slap on the ass. She shuddered, her nerve endings tingling in pleasure.

"And this is for spiking me with those fuck-me shoes of yours." Another slap. Sensations rocketed around to her clit.

"And this is for biting my nipple so I'd come inside you." A third slap nearly sent her over the edge. He licked her stinging flesh.

Frantic, she squirmed in his arms, her oiled skin gliding across his face.

"Is that what you wanted?" He spread her thighs wide and darted his tongue in and out of her throbbing passage. He curled his arm around her leg and rubbed her clit with his hard finger.

She let out a short shriek and he stopped long enough to raise his head. "Sound waves travel farther over water. Too bad you don't have a kimono hem to bite."

But she did have a towel and stuffed a corner inside her mouth. Just in time, too, because he sent his tongue deeper inside her vagina than she thought possible and she crested the highest wave she'd ever ridden. Tumbling and gasping, her undulating body rode the breakers until coming to a peaceful shore with Rick.

MEG ROLLED OVER, the sun gleaming off her bare breasts. "Now it's your turn."

He tossed his shirt to the deck and shucked his shorts, sighing in relief as his cock sprang free. He tugged her to her feet.

"Rick, I'm naked!" She looked frantically around on the water.

"I find making love so much easier that way." He quickly protected himself and lay on the deck chair. He ran his hand up the outside of her thigh and cupped the firm curve of her bottom. "You have the softest skin, Meg, like warm velvet. I love it when you sink on top of me and I can play with your hard little nipples."

She shook her silky hair free from its ponytail and swung one leg over his waist. A mischievous gleam lit her eyes. Whatever delusions of control he had were floating away, but he was too aroused to care.

She tapped the head of his cock, grinning as it flexed in response. "Too bad you already covered up. We could have had some fun first." She blew on him, the cold air chilling the latex. He shivered and gasped as she rubbed her breasts over him. Her rock-hard nipples scraped along his belly.

He hooked his hands under her arms and dragged her up his body. She leaned forward and sank onto his erection.

"Oh, Meg." It was all he could do to stop from coming right then. He'd been aroused for hours. She moved on him, and he muffled a groan. She was tight and wet, creating a mind-blowing combination of heat and cold as she lifted herself and paused, letting the strong lake breeze chill the lower part of his shaft before enveloping him in her warmth.

Her long, sexy hair blew across her closed eyes, catching on her damp, parted lips.

The boat's rocking drove him deeper into her, her thighs bunching and relaxing as she moved. Her slick body shone in the sunlight, her coral nipples gleaming. He sat up and took one in his mouth, the sun lotion's slightly bitter taste mixing with her salty skin and the underlying sweetness of her flesh.

She contracted around him and shoved him back

onto the lounge, obviously not wanting to lose control yet. "Work below decks, sailor."

"Aye, aye, Cap'n." He decided to do a little swabbing and stroked her clit, enjoying how she clenched around him.

She cupped her breasts, staring at him with a secret smile. "Do you remember that painting from the pillow book where the woman is pleasuring herself?"

"My favorite." The geisha in the painting had the same blissful look as Meg, oblivious to anything but her sensual pleasure. He'd never been with a woman as enthusiastic as she.

Closing her eyes, she undulated on top of his body, teasing and caressing the peaks of her breasts until they were long and swollen. "She had a sex toy, remember?"

"Mmm." A long, carved ivory phallus that slipped into her wet, waiting depths just as he slipped into Meg's.

"Since I don't have mine here…" She trailed off her words suggestively.

"You have one at home?" He gritted his teeth and thrust his hips hard. The idea of her pleasuring herself made him even more aroused. "What does it look like?"

She leaned forward, her coconut-scented breasts gliding across his chest. "Long and hard and thick. You're my toy today." Her green eyes glittered in her heat-flushed face.

"Baby, you can play with me anytime." He

grabbed her ass and angled his erection, surging into her tight warmth.

"When the toy isn't enough, I touch myself." She petted her clit, her fingertips stroking him at the same time. "And I imagine your hard cock driving into me until I come." He obliged, thrusting into her wet depths. Tossing her face to the sun, she melted around him. Sweat beaded on her polished skin while her juices slicked his shaft.

He dug his fingers into her hips and bucked off the chair, the waves of his orgasm buffeting him until he broke free of the sensual undertow.

Meg sighed in pleasure as the final rays of sunset silhouetted Chicago's impressive skyline. Rick pulled her sideways onto his lap, and she nuzzled his bristly jaw. His skin smelled faintly of his cologne and more strongly of sunblock, salt and sunshine.

He wore an unbuttoned blue plaid madras shirt and had pulled on his swimsuit. They had eventually made it into the cool lake water for a swim in between lovemaking sessions, and her damp suit was hanging in the cockpit to dry. She was naked under the thin cotton of her sundress.

They had a perfect view of the 150-foot Ferris wheel crowning Navy Pier, a gargantuan entertainment complex that jutted three thousand feet into Lake Michigan. The upcoming Fourth of July fireworks would be launched from an offshore barge.

A flotilla of small boats as well as larger yachts

bobbed closer to shore. Rick had anchored farther out to avoid the noise and dubious captaining skills of partying boaters. A shadowy cocoon enveloped them, the waves against the hull muting nearby sounds.

"Want some wine?" He picked up his glass of white wine and tipped it against her lips before taking his own sip.

She picked up a chocolate truffle from the box the caterer had packed with their delicious picnic. "Wine, lobster salad, chocolate, sex—what more could a girl ask for on her maiden voyage?"

He gave a half smile at her joke and drank some wine. "Just sex, Meg?"

The chocolate made her mouth gooey and she had to clear her throat several times. Not that she was stalling to think of an answer or anything. "What do you mean?"

Rick set down his glass and stroked her bare arm. "We started off like that at the wedding reception. But that was almost two months ago, and things seem different now. I couldn't stop thinking about you in Hong Kong and could barely concentrate on my work."

Meg took a deep breath. "Me, too. I was writing my article and kept staring off into space wondering how you were."

He nuzzled her neck. "I missed your beautiful face smiling at me, your nose wrinkling when you disagree with me." Meg laughed and he continued, "Even those little freckles across your cheeks."

"My freckles?" Wow, he even liked her freckles. His

candor made her bold. "I've never felt this way about a man before, but I don't know where we're going."

"Someplace new, but we'll figure it out along the way. For now, let's just sail along." He feathered kisses over her cheeks. "One for each freckle."

Meg turned on his lap and straddled him. "Sure you haven't missed any?" She slowly unbuttoned her sundress. "I'd feel tons better if you checked."

Rick gave her a white wolfish grin in the dusk as she shrugged the soft cotton down to puddle around her waist. "It's kinda dark, but I think I found something here." He thumbed her nipples into aching points.

She pressed her breasts against his hand. "Not freckles, but still needing kisses."

"Come back here," he whispered. "I want to play with your breasts."

"I had something different in mind." She braced her hands on his thighs. Inhaling his unique scent, she licked his flat brown nipple and he jerked in surprise. She moved to his other nipple before he could protest and caught it between her upper teeth and tongue.

"Easy, honey." He slipped his hand inside her dress, cupping her breast with his big hand.

"Trying to distract me?" A lake breeze ruffled his wavy hair, silhouetted against the midnight blue sky. His face was shadowed, so she couldn't see his expression.

But she felt his response. His cock flexed under

her belly, reminding her of her ultimate destination. She licked his flat stomach, dipping her tongue into his navel.

He jumped. "Hey, that tickles!"

"Sorry." She blew on his wet skin. He squirmed, his erection straining against the thin nylon of his swim trunks. "You need some more room in those things."

She pulled down his waistband. With her teeth.

The elastic pressed the tip of his cock against his belly. She exhaled a hot breath of air and blew a cold stream across the swollen head. A silvery bead formed, gleaming in the dim light. Slicking her finger in the moisture, she spread it around his hot flesh.

He tipped his head back on the lounger, unsuccessfully fighting a groan. "I give up, baby. I don't care if half the Chicago Yacht Club sails by—I'll go crazy if you don't take me in your mouth."

Meg sat on her heels as he lifted his hips and shoved his swim trunks to his knees. His penis sprung free, tall and straight as the mast on the sailboat. She lowered her head but stopped, a mischievous grin creeping across her face. "First, you have to ask for it like a real sailor."

"And how does a real sailor ask a beautiful woman to make him the happiest man on Lake Michigan?"

"You say, 'Well, blow me down.'"

His surprised laugh turned into a groan as she took his smooth flesh in her mouth. She licked little flicks around his taut head, dipping the tip of her tongue in the tiny slit on top. He rewarded her efforts with another salty droplet, which she swirled around his shaft with her tongue.

"More." He threaded his fingers in her wind-tangled hair, urging her into a slow rhythm. "Like that."

Meg complied, taking him deep into her throat. Her hand cupped the lower half of his shaft and stroked the veins pulsing under her fingers. She decided to try something she'd only read about.

He jackknifed violently. "What was that?"

"Don't you like it?" She'd flipped up her tongue and ran the softer underside over the V-shaped zone near the head of his penis.

"Hell, yeah!"

She grinned and did it again, this time rubbing the bottom of her tongue across him while she twisted her hand. The silky texture and vibrant taste of his skin aroused her so her breath came hot and fast out of her nostrils.

He thrust into her mouth, nearly lifting her off his lap. "No, Meg, stop, I can't take any more." He teetered on the edge. His powerful thigh muscles flexed as he hooked his hands under her arms and dragged her up his body.

She captured his lips with hers, letting him taste his juices on her tongue. She straddled his lap, and he shoved her dress around her waist. "Nothing under your dress?"

"My suit was wet." It had dried hours ago.

He knew that, too, judging by his wicked grin. His long finger dipped into her slick passage and withdrew, moistening her tiny bundle of nerves. "Wet, huh?" He slipped his finger in and out. His callused sailor's thumb stroked her pulsing clit.

Lost in the fog of passion, she let out a loud moan. He grabbed a condom from her beach bag and hurriedly sheathed himself. She turned so his erection pressed against her bottom. "Permission to come aboard, captain?"

"Aye, aye." He snapped her a quick salute as she slowly lowered herself onto his throbbing cock. "Ay-yi-yi."

Using her strong thigh muscles, Meg rode him. Rick quickly caught her rhythm and grasped her hips.

A loud boom broke into their passionate reverie. "What the—" he exclaimed.

"Look." She pointed to the pier. "Fireworks."

"And I thought it was just me."

Peals of giddy laughter burst from her throat. She still couldn't believe they were bobbing along on Lake Michigan, watching world-class pyrotechnics while making their own.

"Hey, do that again." He shifted under her, pushing even farther in.

"You like that?" She squeezed him, shuddering with pleasure at his hard length inside her.

"Mmm." He reached under her skirt and stroked her bare knee, dragging his fingers along the seam where their thighs met. He stopped where her damp folds encased him. "You like that?"

She grabbed his hand to move it a couple inches

to the center, but he didn't budge. "Rick, please." A red starburst detonated above the lake.

He leaned forward and nuzzled her neck, finally strumming her tiny knot. Waves of heat rippled through her whole body until she quivered above him. He lit a fire in her, melting her inhibitions.

Meg opened her eyes as the grand finale started. The barge had lit a long chain of low-exploding fireworks. "Hey, does that remind you of anything?" Behind her, Rick rocked inside her.

His eyes flew open as he stared blearily at the display. Streams of white light gushed upward, jetting into the night sky.

He focused long enough to laugh. A pink flower firework bloomed high overhead. "Time for you to fall into my hands, cherry blossom."

Speeding his thrusts, he caressed her until she burst into a thousand glittering fragments that rained down to ignite his own explosive climax.

10

MEG HUNG UP HER office phone Monday after a strange conversation with the university printing service. They had insisted the costs listed in Nigel's budget for the art exhibit booklet were more than double what they had quoted him. Not looking forward to hearing Nigel's asinine explanation, she dropped the budget on her desk.

Time for her morning e-mail fix. She opened her computer's inbox and groaned. As usual, her mother had sent several digital photos of generic-looking middle-aged Japanese men. She rapidly skipped through all but the last e-mail, which had no photo attached.

Dear Megan, let me know which successful young man you'd like to e-mail. They are all eager to meet you.

Meg rolled her eyes at the computer screen. "Well, that makes one of us."

She was about to click the delete button when she took a second look at the screen.

Your father and I will stop over in Chicago Thursday on our way to New York. The Regent Hotel shuttle will pick us up from the airport, so we will call you when we get settled. Love, your mother.

"Holly." No response. "Holly!" Meg raised her voice. Her student worker had performed in another rock concert and was still recovering from the auditory assault.

Her assistant popped her head around the corner. Today her hair was black with cobalt-blue streaks. "Whoa, what happened to your desk? It's even messier than usual."

Meg shrugged. She could have sworn she'd at least neatened the files and various scrolls before leaving last night. "Probably the cleaning service knocked them around while dusting. Do I have any appointments Thursday afternoon?"

"Nope, looks good." Holly strolled into the office, her long blue tunic flowing after her. "Why? Is your sizzlin' hot boyfriend coming over for some hooky-nooky?"

"You're awful." Meg blushed but laughed all the same. "No, my parents are coming to town and I have some errands to run."

"Are you doing the big 'meet-the-parents' dinner?"

"Are you kidding? If my mother knew I was seeing someone, she'd be planning our wedding already. Deleting those e-mail photos is a lot easier than giving her a real, live, oxygen-breathing man to focus on."

"Oh, did she send you more photos?" Holly closed the office door and pulled a chair over to sit next to Meg. "Open those bad boys!"

Meg clicked the first one and they both groaned. "Is that tape on his glasses?" Meg asked.

"Next!" Bachelor Number Two didn't impress Holly, either. "What a butterball. He barely fits in the photo. Who's next?"

"Ah." They looked at each other and nodded wisely. Bachelor Three was prettier than Meg and Holly combined. "His mother will wait forever for grandchildren," Meg commented. Holly snickered.

"And on to unlucky Number Four. Four is the number of death in Japan, you know." Meg clicked open the final photo.

"Freaky." Holly grimaced.

"What, the number or the guy?"

"Both. That one looks like an Asian version of Nigel."

Meg peered at the screen. "He does, doesn't he?"

"That same snooty look, the beady eyes and the prissy lips. Wait. Is that jacket tweed?" Holly turned to Meg. "Do Japanese guys wear tweed?"

"No, not usually." Meg shrugged. "Maybe he used to live in England or Canada."

"Bzzzzt. Thank you for playing, Nigel-look-alike-*san. Sayonara!*" Holly sent Nigel's Japanese double to the trash bin. "What's the difference between this guy and Nigel?"

Meg caught her breath from laughing. "I don't know. What *is* the difference?"

"Bachelor Number Four has *yen* in the bank and Nigel has a *yen* for you!"

"No way. Nigel?" Meg thought it was more likely Nigel had a *yen* for the pillow book and the dough he could get for it.

"He's been asking about you all the time. You know, where you are, what you're doing with the pillow book, that kind of thing."

"Well, these guys can keep their *yen* far from me, money and otherwise." Meg closed her program, emphatically clicking *yes* to permanently delete the e-mails.

"Seriously, Meg?" Holly cleared her throat.

Meg looked up in surprise at her assistant's unusually solemn tone. "What is it?"

Holly looked at the office door to make sure they were alone. "My friend Saffron came by so we could walk to the *BITChi* sorority meeting together, and we ran into Nigel as we were leaving, and Saffron said…" Holly fidgeted with the huge safety pins holding her tunic together.

"What?"

Holly's words rushed out. "She said Nigel's aura is black around the edges."

"A black aura?" Meg had heard plenty of complaints about Nigel's unpleasant personality and sloppy scholarship, but this was a first.

"Saffron says not to trust him." Holly shrugged and stared at her maroon fingernails. "She's never wrong."

"I'll be careful," she promised.

Holly smiled, her tough-girl facade falling away for a second. "Cool. Thanks for not laughing."

Meg shooed her out the door. "Don't worry about me. Nigel may have a black aura, but *I* have a black belt."

RICK REACHED for Meg in his sleep, awakening when he couldn't find her. He cracked open one eye and squinted at the alarm clock on the heavy Greek nightstand. Five a.m. and Meg wasn't in bed.

They'd had a leisurely dinner interrupted by several annoying voice mail messages from her boss asking about things that could have waited until tomorrow. After she'd finally turned off her phone, they'd torn each other's clothes off and spent all night making love, including one wet and steamy interlude in the whirlpool tub. He pulled on some shorts and went to look for her.

She was in the living room wearing the peach silk nightgown he'd bought her in Hong Kong. It looked great on her, but her ubiquitous cotton gloves spoiled the whole effect. "Meg?"

"Hmm?" She turned a page carefully, engrossed in the pillow book. Again. She jotted several notes and showed no signs of paying any attention to him.

"Megan!" His words came out sharper than he intended.

"What?" She raised her eyebrows. "Is something wrong?"

"No, um…" Now he felt like an idiot. He looked out the wall of windows above the lake. "I thought we could enjoy the sunrise together."

"Sure." She blinked a couple times and stood. Pulling off her gloves, she yawned. "I usually only see the sunrise when I stay up working all night."

He guided her to the windows where streaks of pink lightened the eastern horizon, turning the black lake bluish-gray. Her silky dark hair tickled his chest. They watched the sky in silence for a few minutes, his arms wrapped around her.

Meg twitched slightly, probably eager to return to her studying. He didn't want to lose her attention yet. "Maybe sometime we can see the sun set over the Pacific Ocean. My parents live close to the beach."

"Your parents?" She tipped up her face. "You don't talk too much about them."

He shrugged. "Not much to say. They're perpetually teetering on the brink of divorce but neither is willing to give up half of their assets. Dad's law firm made a boatload of money and he wasn't about to let mom have half. California community property law was the only thing keeping them together. Sure wasn't concern for me and my sister."

She patted his forearm. "Why did you guys move there anyway?"

Rick let go of her and turned toward the kitchen. "Want some orange juice?"

"Okay." Meg watched him go, bemused by his sudden withdrawal. He poured two glasses and set them on the breakfast bar. Meg gave the beautiful sunrise one last glance and walked into the darkness where Rick waited.

She sipped at the OJ and nibbled at some leftover raspberry coffeecake. "I never liked California much. The traffic was worse than Tokyo and I wasn't exactly a beach bunny."

"It took me a while to get used to it after we moved. But five-year-olds are adaptable, and it's not like I had a choice."

Her mouth full of coffeecake, Meg could only nod in agreement. What kid did have any choice?

"We moved because my father had an affair with the next door neighbor's wife."

She choked on her mouthful of pastry and grabbed the juice to wash it down. "That's terrible." So Captain Bligh had gone sailing for illicit booty.

"Mom was humiliated. He insisted it was the first time he'd ever strayed, and she forgave him. He accepted a job transfer to Southern California, and we left Chicago to start over. Left my grandparents, my aunts and uncles, and my cousins, who were my best friends." He stared unseeing out the window.

"Sometimes a fresh start is best." She felt silly, relying on tired clichés, but she couldn't think of what to say.

"He needed plenty of fresh starts. He had grass stains on his clothes from all the times my mother chucked them on the front lawn." Rick barked a bitter laugh. "One time, she followed him after work with my sister and me sitting in the backseat of our wood-paneled station wagon. Found him at a bar with a blond secretary from the law office. She shoved us at the woman, saying if she wanted my dad, she could take his kids, too. Mom took off up the Pacific Coast Highway and made it to Monterey before she even bothered to call the next day."

"Wow." With a cheat for a father and a drama queen for a mother, no wonder Rick was wary of love.

"The only good times my sister and I had were our summers in Chicago. My grandpa did everything for me that my dad should have. But he was keeping secrets, too."

"And your grandmother never knew about the pillow book?"

"I asked her last week about any Japanese souvenirs he'd brought her and she showed me a tea set and an old kimono." He laughed. "I couldn't quite bring myself to ask about erotic Japanese drawings."

"He must have wanted to keep it, Rick. He could have left it at the Art Institute, dropped it at the Chicago Public Library donation desk. He could have burned it and no one would have been the wiser."

"One of Japan's priceless antiquities gone up in smoke."

She shrugged, refusing to let him distract her from

the real issue. "Along with thousands of others, but that's not the point. Look, your grandfather was young and alone in a foreign country for the first time. My own father was a twenty-two-year-old sailor stationed in Tokyo when he met my mother."

"My grandfather was dating my grandmother. They were practically engaged." He shoved his hands into his robe pockets. "I never figured him for a cheater. My father, sure, but not his dad."

"Didn't you tell me your grandmother was sixteen and he was nineteen when he was drafted? She was still a kid and he was a grown man. And men of that era, especially honorable ones like your grandfather, wouldn't have pressured a young girl to compromise herself before marriage. Maybe he spent time with someone in Japan." There, that was about as delicate as she could put it. Her feet were exhausted from all the tiptoeing.

"I guess." He still wore a troubled look. "But did he buy that book? Was it a gift?"

"I haven't found any clues from my research, but I'll let you know if I do."

He pulled himself back from wherever his thoughts had wandered. "How is your research going? Did you hear from that art journal?"

"My research is going fine but I haven't heard from the editor yet." She knew he was only being polite. He'd looked so sad discussing the book that she didn't want him to feel bad anymore. Somewhere during their summer fling, Rick had become very important to her, more important than she wanted to consider.

If she was in love with him, as she'd suspected since their sailing trip, she didn't really want to deal with that. Thinking about when he went back to California made her stomach hurt, so she changed the subject whenever he mentioned the end of summer.

She reached across the breakfast bar and took his hand. "Let's go back to bed."

"I'm not tired." He hopped up from the stool and kissed her, his breath citrusy and tangy.

She winked at him. "Neither am I."

MEG REACHED OVER to pick up her ringing phone. "Megan O'Malley," she said, fanning herself. The late afternoon sun always heated her office to a broil.

"Hello, Dr. O'Malley," a female voice asked. "This is Sylvia Sutter. I'm an editor with *Asian Art Exploration.* We had talked a few weeks ago about the possibility of publishing your journal article on a little-known, historically significant pillow book."

"Yes, hello, Sylvia." Meg sat up straight and grabbed a pen to take notes. "The artwork is spectacular and the margin notes by the original noblewoman owner are very enlightening as to the cultural mores of the Late Edo period." There, that should sound sufficiently pedantic.

"It did sound intriguing when we first discussed it, and one of our other articles fell through for an upcoming issue. Would you be able to send us your article within ten days so we can start sending it out for peer review?"

Meg's pen screeched to a halt, leaving a jagged black line. "Ten days?" Her parents were coming, she had the printer's deadline for the exhibition program plus a million little details to take care of…

"The professors we're sending it to are both leaving on a research trip shortly, so we're in a time crunch, sorry to say." The editor did sound apologetic, but Meg knew she didn't have a choice if she wanted that slot.

"That will be fine." She injected an optimistic tone into her voice that she didn't quite feel. "I've read your journal for years, and it's very exciting to be considered for publication."

"How kind of you." The editor went on to discuss specific guidelines for the article with Meg jotting everything down. Good thing she had written an outline and started on a rough draft.

They finally hung up and she broke into a wide grin. Tight deadline or no, it was a prestigious journal, and she had Rick to thank for it. Grabbing her phone, she dialed him to arrange a little private celebration. Maybe flipping through the pillow book together would stimulate all kinds of new ideas.

11

MEG SHIFTED HER GROCERY bags to one hand and cursed as her stubborn deadbolt stuck tight. A smidgen of humidity and her apartment was Fort Knox. Without the money, unfortunately. She gave the door a front snap kick. The miserable thing finally opened just as her phone rang.

She tossed her bags on the narrow bamboo hall table and grabbed the receiver. "Hello?"

"Michiko-*chan!*" Her mother's soft accent rolled through the phone.

"Ma! How was your trip?" Meg automatically slipped into Japanese.

"Long, but I managed to sleep for several hours. Your father and I got settled into our hotel. A suite, too." Kazuko Yamamoto O'Malley had grown up desperately poor during the chaotic post-war occupation of Japan and now relished her luxuries.

"Sounds nice." The Regent Hotel was only a few blocks from her apartment.

"Very nice." Her mother continued without pausing for breath. "You spend the night here. I have appointments at the hotel spa for massage and facial. Have you been taking care of your skin? I hope you have been wearing your sunblock. Too many freckles already."

Meg choked back laughter. "I always use sunblock. I put it on all over when I'm in the sun." She happened to know the best sunblock applier in Chicago.

"Good." Her mother was mollified. For the time being, anyway. "So you come tonight?"

"Yes, Ma."

"Is that my Meggie?" her dad bellowed. After a brief tussle for the phone, he came on the line. "Darlin' girl, tell your weary old da you have his bottle of Bushmills ready."

"Hi, Dad. It's right here, waiting for the mail."

"Rip open the box. We'll come over for a wee drink and whisk you off to dinner and a day of feminine folderol."

Meg laughed. She was perfectly capable of meeting them at the hotel, but her dad always insisted on visiting her apartment to check her door and window locks. With them living so far away, he liked picturing her puttering safe and happy around her place. "See you around six-thirty?"

"Great!" Her dad blew her a kiss over the phone and hung up.

She had an hour for a quick dash-and-stash. Throw out any incriminating empty wrappers, tuck Rick's razor and shaving cream in the corner of the linen closet and shove his extra pair of sneakers under her bed. He wouldn't need any of his gear tonight.

Rick planned to eat dinner at his grandmother's assisted-living apartment and help her sort through more attic boxes he'd brought over. Meg had offered to come along in case another amazing Japanese antiquity popped up, but Rick had laughed and said one big surprise like that was enough.

Maybe next week she could meet his grandmother and talk to her about the pillow book. Rick might want to show her a less explicit painting, like the geisha and the cherry blossoms. Another pretty painting illustrated the fable of the maiden and the enchanted prince trapped in the body of a stallion. Mrs. Sokol didn't need to know the maiden broke the spell sexually.

Rick had certainly developed a healthy admiration for the Japanese erotic paintings. After her parents left for New York on Monday, Meg would give him another private lesson in art appreciation.

RICK KNOCKED ON Meg's apartment door. He wanted to surprise her, and her upstairs neighbor had let him in the lobby door.

"Rick!" She looked stunned. "What are you doing here?"

"Grandma was too tired to visit any more today."

"Is she okay?" Her green eyes widened in concern.

"Yeah, but the heat is bothering her. She has brand-new central air-conditioning but she doesn't like to waste electricity. I made her turn it on anyway." He brought out the bouquet he'd hidden behind him.

"Pink roses!" She grabbed the plastic bouquet

sleeve and inhaled deeply. "Oh, look, there's a bunch of cherry blossoms in them, too."

"Sorry the cherry blossoms are only silk, but the florists couldn't get any real ones." He'd offered them a bundle to find some, too.

She grinned. "Of course not. They only bloom in the spring. I'll put the roses in some water." She glanced over her shoulder into the living room.

"Am I interrupting anything?" He followed her into her tiny foyer.

"No, of course not."

"Good." He grabbed her shoulders and kissed her hard, nudging her lips with his tongue until she opened to him.

She sucked him deep into her mouth and swirled her tongue around his. The bouquet whacked his shoulder as she threw her arms around him. The dizzying scent of roses surrounded them. He wanted to strew the velvety pink petals across her bed and lay her in their midst.

"Meggie?"

The bouquet dropped from her hand on to the floor, and she jumped away from him as if he'd poked her with a thorn.

A hulking redheaded man stood in the entrance to the living room. "I heard voices, and then I didn't hear anything."

"Meg?" Rick looked at her. The guy was in his fifties and almost as tall as he was. A cunning look shone from his green eyes.

"Dad." Meg bit her bottom lip, unfortunately drawing attention to its kiss-puffed state.

"Your father?" Obviously the source of Meg's own green eyes.

"Yes. Dad, this is Rick Sokol. Rick, this is my father, Sean O'Malley."

Thank God he hadn't had a chance to put his hands on her ass, or even worse, her breasts. "Pleased to meet you, sir." Rick extended his hand and was relieved when the older man shook it.

"Same here." He gestured into the living room. "I'll let your mother know you have company."

"I thought your parents were arriving late," Rick muttered, running his fingers through his hair.

She shrugged. "They got an earlier flight. Since you were with your grandmother, I didn't think it mattered." She picked up the roses.

"Michiko!" A tiny Japanese woman hurried around the corner. "Why is your handsome guest still standing in the hall? Come in, come in." She took his arm with a surprising strong grip and tugged him into the living room.

"Mom, this is Rick Sokol," Meg called over her shoulder as she carried the roses into the kitchen.

"Rick." Her mother pronounced the "r" carefully as she practically shoved him onto Meg's couch. "I am Kazuko O'Malley, Michiko's mother. And you are Michiko's…?" Her voice trailed off as she invited him to fill in the blank.

"Friend."

"Oh." Her round face drooped. Sean gave a loud snort and said a couple words in Japanese. It was obviously an explanation of how he'd been kissing Meg, because Kazuko clapped her hands in delight, her brown eyes sparkling. "Excuse me, please. I will help with the flowers." She gave her husband a look and trotted off.

Sean sat in an armchair across from him. A flurry of Japanese conversation spilled from the tiny kitchen. "So, Rick, is it?"

"Yes, sir."

"Tell me about yourself." The older man's pleasant smile didn't quite reach his eyes.

Rick took a deep breath and described how his private investigations agency specialized in corporate espionage, employee misconduct and internal investigations.

"You started that business yourself?"

"Yes. I majored in engineering and business administration at UCLA." Her dad didn't need to know he'd minored in frat parties and sorority girls.

"Ah." Her father nodded thoughtfully. "And did you know Meggie when she attended USC?" His relaxed pose didn't disguise his intense interest.

"No, we met this summer at our friends' wedding and again when she appraised something of my grandmother's." Sweat trickled down his spine. He hadn't been put on the spot like this since his senior prom. His date's father had been a sniper for the LAPD who just happened to be cleaning his rifle when Rick arrived.

"Dad!" Meg set a crystal vase full of his pink roses on the coffee table. "Enough. I'm a big girl now."

"I know, darlin'." He patted her cheek. "But even though you're a big girl doesn't mean your da can't have a friendly chat with your young man."

"Sean, I hope you are making our guest welcome." Her mother's coffee-brown eyes narrowed in suspicion. Rick suspected Kazuko was the Japanese version of a steel magnolia. A steel cherry blossom?

"Of course, darlin'. A bit of business talk." Her dad held out his hands in a pose of innocence.

Meg perched on the couch arm next to her dad. Rick tried to keep his eyes off the smooth expanse of thigh disappearing under her tight white shorts. "If you're talking business, Rick's trying to get an in with some American-based Japanese companies to contract their security work. Feel free to pick my dad's brain. Or what's left of it." She grinned, ruffling Sean's salt-and-paprika hair.

"Meg…" Rick shifted on the couch. "I'm sure your father doesn't want to talk shop on his visit."

"Let the men talk business if they want. I want to see your wardrobe." Kazuko beckoned to her daughter in the Asian way, her palm facing down.

"Mom, I have plenty of things to wear." She rolled her eyes, as she must have when she was a teenager living at home.

"You may not need my help to find a nice young man, but you still need my help with your clothes." She held up her tiny hand, stopping Meg's protest midword. "You and I are going shopping this weekend—and not at those stores with old clothes!"

"Vintage clothes are hot now."

"Men like to see ladies in new outfits, not something from a thrift store!" Kazuko sniffed and marched into Meg's bedroom, presumably to sort through her closet. He tried to remember if he'd left his things lying around. Surely Meg would have removed any evidence.

"Dad, save me." She clutched him in mock distress.

"Sorry, dear. Your mother's talked of nothing but shopping on the Magnificent Mile since we landed."

"Oh, well. Maybe she'll stop e-mailing me photos every day."

Sean rolled his eyes. "Can't blame you for ducking those namby-pambies your mother digs up. At least you have a red-blooded man like this fella, not a bespectacled bean-counter."

"Dad!" She shot to her bare feet, a peachy flush spreading across her cheeks. Taking a deep breath, she narrowed her eyes in unconscious imitation of her mother. "By the way, Dad, Rick and I went to a benefit for an Asian battered women's shelter, and I thought you and Mom might want to make a donation. Their budget is terribly small."

"I think our New York office has some older computers and filing cabinets." His green eyes twinkled.

"I was talking about a personal donation from *you*. Since I don't see any older computers or filing cabinets in your luggage, how about a check?"

He grinned and patted her knee. "The checkbook's

in your mother's purse. Fill one out, and I'll sign it. Just leave enough in the account to leave the lights on at home."

"Thanks, Dad." She kissed him on the cheek and followed her mother into the bedroom.

"Anything to make my darlin' girl happy. Don't you agree?" Sean's eyes hardened.

"Oh, absolutely," Rick hastened to agree. "Her happiness is very important to me. More important than my own." He stopped in surprise. When had that become the truth? Maybe when he had to leave her for his Hong Kong trip. Would she be able to travel with him on his next one?

"Good to hear. This calls for a drink. I know Meggie has some special whiskey set aside for me." He stopped, one red eyebrow raised. "You do like Bushmills, don't you?"

"My favorite." How could he not like it? He smiled at the memory of Meg slamming her whiskey at the Palmer House bar.

"On the rocks?" Sean called from the kitchen.

Rick knew this was a test, too. "Straight, no water."

"Good man." Sean handed him a tumbler. "Poured you a double." The tiny wicker chair creaked in protest as Sean settled his bulk into it. "Ever done business in Japan before?"

"No, only in Hong Kong and southern China."

"Similar, but not exactly alike. Who are you trying to woo?" He gave Rick a mischievous grin. "Besides my daughter, that is?"

Rick sipped his whiskey and avoided Sean's stare for a second. If Meg were "wooed" any harder, they'd never leave the bedroom. "Various companies, but Fujigawa-Denki Corporation is my main target. Their North American headquarters are in Southern California."

"Fujigawa, eh? Those fellas are tricky. My company dealt with them last year and they nearly left us bloody."

Rick nodded. "Their electronics components are top-notch, but they're unhappy with their current security company, which got some bad press."

"Cardinal sin number one for a Japanese business. Never, ever embarrass the company." The older man drummed his fingers on the armrest. "And your contact?"

"He was making some progress until he got into a car accident on the Santa Monica freeway last week."

Sean shook his head. "Bad luck. You're back at square one unless you find someone else. With your permission, I'd like to help."

Rick hated to ask for assistance. He prided himself in not needing anyone's help, but he desperately needed to make up for lost time. "I'd be grateful. I've wanted to expand further into the defense contractor segment for some time."

The older man's green eyes brightened. "You've got a security clearance?"

"Yes, one of my other DOD clients required that."

"And who would that client be?"

Rick grinned. "You know I can't say, sir."

"Hell, no." He guffawed and slapped his knee, the chair squeaking plaintively. "An old sailor like me should know better than to ask."

Meg came into the living room and sat next to Rick on the couch. "Mom's going to rest for a while. I think my closet sent her into shock."

Sean blew her a kiss and picked up the phone. "Meggie dear, let me know what your long distance bill is. I'll pay for the call."

"No, I will." Rick wasn't about to let her dad cover his tab when Sean was doing him a favor.

Sean nodded and turned his attention to the phone, breaking into a stream of fluent Japanese. He covered the receiver. "My secretary's getting me the number for an executive at Fujigawa-Denki." He wrote the number on a piece of scrap paper and hung up.

He dialed and winked at them. "Ah, yes, *konichi-wa.*" He dragged out a few sentences, speaking in Japanese and stepped onto the small balcony.

Meg patted Rick's knee, wanting to kiss him again but reluctant to exhibit any more public displays of affection with her parents right there. Rick smiled down at her and covered her hand with his. "I'm glad to meet your parents, sweetheart. They're really great."

"They are." Meg rested her head on his shoulder for a minute, contentment gliding over her. Her parents' visits always made her feel safe and secure as they fussed over her and pampered her, but this time her happiness was even greater.

She stole a peek up at Rick. It was because of him. Their relationship had developed into something special since it's purely physical beginning. He'd slowly worn down her defenses with his gifts. Not just flowers and sailing trips, but his gift of listening to her complain and then teasing her out of her grumpy moods. His gift of making love to her and loving her. She bolted upright from his side. Loving her?

"What, honey?" He squeezed her hand.

"Nothing," she answered absently, her mind still turning over the thought that had bubbled up from the back of her mind. They'd never said they loved each other, but she wasn't surprised, considering his childhood and her previous sad excuse for a relationship.

She'd never felt like this about a man before. Was it love? With nothing to compare it to, it was hard to tell.

Sean finished his phone call. "Luck of the Irish comes through again, dearie."

"Blarney-kisser," she retorted, stealing Rick's glass and swigging some whiskey.

"And who was the man who held you upside down so you could kiss the Blarney stone?"

Meg raised the glass in a toast. "You, my dear Dad."

"Damn straight." Sean turned to Rick. "I talked to the Fujigawa fella and told him to expect a proposal from you. I'll give you his e-mail and fax number so you can get the man up to speed."

"Thank you so much, Sean. I appreciate it." Rick grinned in relief. Meg knew he'd spent hours on the phone trying to salvage the situation.

"Anything for a friend of Meggie's." Sean sipped his whiskey, his eyes crafty. "Just one thing. In order to get you an in with them, I might have told a wee fib or so."

"Dad?" Meg narrowed her eyes at her father. His impish expression boded no good.

"They wondered, very politely, mind you, why I was sticking my long Irish nose into your business. Soooo, I told them you were marrying my daughter."

12

"SO WHEN ARE YOU marrying this man?"

Meg choked on her passion-fruit smoothie, dribbling orange globs on the pristine white spa robe. Her mother made a *tsking* sound and handed her a napkin, her own robe still immaculate.

"I'm not marrying Rick." Even if she'd entertained any crazy notion about marrying him, the stunned look on his face was enough to quash that idea. Her dad had roared with laughter and poured him another whiskey. Rick had impressed him so much that her father had invited him to dinner at the steakhouse they always frequented. Meg had never been on a double date with her parents, but they'd all had a great evening.

"If you are foolish enough to pass up that rich, handsome, tall American, your aunt Kimiko's son's wife has a nice cousin. He works as an accountant for the Bank of Japan." Her mother reclined on her spa lounge chair, her round face serene under its green seaweed mask.

"No, Mom, don't send me his photo or e-mail address. I won't ever contact him."

"Why are you always so rude? He's practically family."

"You know what they say about marrying relatives, Mom. The kids turn out funny-looking." Meg sipped her smoothie, pleased at finally scoring a point.

Her mother narrowed her eyes and deliberately relaxed her expression, not wanting to crack the face-mask. "I want what's best for you."

"And what's best for me is to get married? Did Aunt Kimiko call me Christmas cake again?" *Christmas cake* was an unkind way of referring to unmarried Japanese women. Christmas cake might be a sweet, delicious treat, but nobody wanted it after the twenty-fifth. And since Meg had passed her twenty-fifth birthday four years previously, some of her mother's friends definitely thought her sell-by date had come and gone.

"No. She did not make that mistake again." Her voice was as steely as the samurai sword on the wall at home. "After what happened to Kimiko's own daughter, she does not have the nerve."

Meg muffled her snicker behind her glass. Aunt Kimiko's daughter had been betrothed at the ripe old age of nineteen to a forty-year-old family friend. Instead of buckling down to a typically loveless domestic existence, she had broken her engagement and moved to San Francisco with her Californian-born English teacher named Barb.

"They have nothing to do with this." Mom sat up and frowned, mask be damned. "It is because of *you.*

You were pleased about your friend getting married, but also a bit envious. So, I thought you wanted a wedding of your own. And I know plenty of nice Japanese men."

What? She'd pushed away any minute, infinitesimal traces of envy by joking and complaining about Rey's wedding. But her mother had read her like a *manga* comic book. Meg tried to choose her words carefully. "Even if I wanted to marry someone, it probably wouldn't be a Japanese man. You understand, don't you? After all, you and Dad have been happily married for thirty years and he's not Japanese."

"Well…" Her mother's voice trailed off.

Meg set her glass down with a click. "Well, what? You're not happy?"

"Oh, yes, we are now, but in the beginning, it was difficult."

"Difficult?" This was the first Meg had heard about any problems in her parent's marriage. Her dad was a high-powered executive and her mother seemed content to run the home and support her dad's career.

"My father disowned me when I accepted your father's proposal. Your grandfather Kenji was a proud man. He remembered the war years and the occupation…he believed Americans were immoral, rude and disrespectful." She sighed. "And the women who dated American sailors were held in low esteem."

"How did you fix it?" Meg remembered her grandfather as a mild-mannered, patient man who had taken the time to teach her traditional Japanese calligraphy.

"You were born. Your grandmother sweetly and gently badgered him until he attended your naming ceremony. You were only seven days old and he held you for the first time. When he heard we named you Michiko, his eyes filled with tears. He had always been devoted to the Empress Michiko."

"That's so sweet, Mom." She'd never known about their family falling-out. What if Grandfather Kenji had never relented? She would have grown up never knowing her Japanese relatives. Maybe her parents' marriage would have buckled under the strain of isolation and estrangement. They all might have descended into the bickering and sniping that must have marred Rick's childhood.

"So come home with your father and me. If you don't want a Japanese husband, your father knows plenty of other eligible businessmen who live in Tokyo."

Meg rolled her eyes. "Mom, what am I supposed to do if I move back to Japan? Be an office lady at some Japanese art auction house?" Office ladies in Japan sat at desks all day clipping papers together and serving tea, whiling away their days until they snagged a husband. "I won't find a decent apartment and you know women are only paid about half of what a man earns."

"You could have your old room…" Her mother trailed off as Meg made a face. "All right, Michiko-*chan*." Her mother sighed. "I miss having you nearby so I can see you more often."

"Oh, Mom, I miss you, too." Meg reached over and patted her mother's hand, the delicate bones and tendons crisscrossing under the pampered skin. "Maybe you can come visit me without Dad. Or fly with him to Europe on his business trips and catch a flight to Chicago."

"Travel without your father?" Her mother's eyes widened. "I don't know…."

"You can do it. After all, you were the traditional Japanese girl who defied her father to marry an American sailor."

"Hmmph. Your grandfather would laugh to see us now. Me the traditional mother, and you the rebellious daughter."

"It's a Zen-like concept, isn't it? What goes around comes around."

"Zen? I'll show you Zen!" Her mom swiped at her, forgetting her matronly Japanese dignity and spilling her own slushy strawberry drink on her robe.

"THAT CHINESE CARRYOUT makes the best General Tso's chicken in Chicago." Meg licked her chopsticks and patted her lips with a paper napkin. A half-dozen white containers were strewn across her office desk.

"We could have gone someplace nice…" Rick finished his Tsingtao beer, trying to cool the hot pepper burn. Eating out of cardboard boxes in her tiny university office was not his idea of a romantic lunch. And they hadn't even been alone since nearby students had detected the food's delicious aroma and mooched several helpings.

"I told you when you called earlier that I was too busy to take a long lunch," she said firmly, before smiling. "Besides, all the Chinese students from the university go to the Golden Palace. Reminds them of home."

Rick could believe that, having eaten similar meals in Hong Kong. Meg had ordered their lunch in Cantonese. A far cry from the expensive steakhouse her parents had taken them to on Friday. "How was your parents' visit?"

"We had a great time, despite my mother dragging me into every boutique on North Michigan Avenue. I think the shopping alone managed to convince her to visit more often."

"I enjoyed meeting your parents." Except for the awkward moment when her dad had teased him about proposing to Meg, their visit had gone smoothly.

"They liked you, especially my mother." She made a face. "She spent my whole relaxing spa day grilling me over our plans for the future."

Meg had ducked discussing the future with him as well, but he didn't have any good ideas, either. Once summer was over and his grandmother's house was up for sale, he'd have to get back to L.A. and Meg had her full course load to teach. "What did you tell her?"

"I told her you lived in California and I lived in Chicago and the last time I checked, they were pretty far apart."

Rick rolled his chopsticks between his fingers. He did have a life back in L.A. His condo near the ocean, his business offices, most of his clients. But no one to come home to.

Meg was fussing with the leftover napkins. "Mix one Japanese mother, one unmarried daughter and a handsome, sexy, eligible man, and you're bound to get some maternal pressure. But we're off the hook. My dad has a meeting in New York tomorrow." She stood and brushed crumbs from her lemon-yellow pants.

Despite her wry comments, she looked wistful. Sometimes having a taste of family was enough to make you lonely when they left.

Just like he was relieved to have Meg all to himself again. Meg's parents were great, but meeting them had pointed out the huge gulf between their family life and his. The last time he'd felt like he'd had a real home was when he stayed with his grandparents.

No, that wasn't right. He fumbled the chopsticks, dropping one in surprise. He always felt like he had a home when Meg was with him, and it had been too long since they'd spent any time alone. "When can you come over tonight?"

"Tonight? Oh, Rick, I can't." She packed up the leftovers into a paper bag. "Between the long holiday weekend and my mom and dad's visit, I've lost too much work time as it is. My journal article is due the day after tomorrow."

"Why can't you work at the condo?" Meg handed him the bag and he guessed that was his cue to take off.

"You know why." She laughed. "I study the pillow book, you study me studying the book, and then I'm not studying the book anymore."

He threw away some paper napkins. "Sorry if I'm such a distraction."

She gave him a cool look. "Aren't I a distraction for you, too? After all, you have your business to run and your grandmother's house to renovate."

"Yes, but I'm not too busy to spend time with you." His secretary managed office matters and his grandmother's neighbor Bob had recommended a dependable contractor.

"Good for you. To whom do you think I should delegate my responsibility for the upcoming exhibit? Nigel? No, he's my boss and delegated it to me. And how about the journal article I'm working on? Maybe Holly can do that for me. Except she doesn't speak Japanese!" Her face flushed deep pink and her green eyes threw sparks at him.

"Hey, I'm trying to help you out here. There's no reason why you should get stuck with all this work. Look how stressed out you are." He stood up from her uncomfortable visitor's chair and rubbed her tight shoulders.

Meg heaved a deep sigh, her muscles finally loosening. "If you've got any ideas, I'd like to hear them. All my graduate assistants are away for the summer and no one else can write my article." His big body was hot behind her, his solidity comforting. She knew she was getting too worked up, but she couldn't figure a way to make things better.

"If you're unhappy here, you should consider another job."

Her muscles knotted again and she faced him. "Another job?"

"A smaller university or college with less pressure to publish." He wrapped his arms around her waist. "Somewhere where you'd have more free time."

Free time, presumably for long romantic lunches and lots of afternoon quickies. "While that does sound good, there aren't a lot of those jobs around."

"Or if you don't want to stay in academic life, you could get a job in the business world. Lots of companies need experts in Asian languages and cultures. Like my company," he finished casually.

"Your company? You want me to work for you as a private investigator?" She was much too blunt to be a good dissembler. "I thought you said I didn't hide my emotions well."

"No, not as an investigator. You don't blend in." She gave him a narrow stare. He obviously read her emotions because he started to look nervous. "You know what I mean, Meg. You're so beautiful, anyone would remember you."

"So what fabulous job are you offering me?" she asked, not bothering to modify her skeptical tone.

"In my office. Translations, interpreting, lots of interesting things like that. And we could travel together, Asia, Europe—"

All sorts of alarms rang in her head. "You want me to be your secretary? An office lady?" She would have stayed in Japan if she'd wanted that.

"No, of course not." He stepped quickly to face her. "This is a way we can be together in L.A. I'd cover your expenses while you looked for a university job, if you even wanted to. What do you think?"

Meg looked at him in dismay. It sounded as if he were paying her to move to L.A. with him. Would she merit a nice allowance if she kept him happy? Ugh.

Being a professional girlfriend was not how she had wanted to continue their relationship into fall. But better to know that now than later after she'd actually told him she loved him. "I already have a job. I'm sorry it's not as fancy as you think it should be, but it's mine and I keep it without kowtowing to some guy."

"How about Nigel?" He crossed his arms over his chest. "As far as I've seen, you've never stood up to him, never told him where he could stick his ridiculous tasks."

"That's different. Once I get tenure—"

"You'll still be the junior member in the department and nothing will change. You're already an office lady, only with a Ph.D. after your name."

For once her multilingual swearword vocabulary failed her. "Do you know how hard I've worked to get to this point? Nine years of college and graduate school, dozens of semesters teaching bored undergrads, eleven interviews to get a tenure-track position, and you call me that?"

"Meg, there are other jobs—"

She shook her head. "Do you want to give up your career, give up everything you worked for your whole adult life?" She jabbed a finger at him. "Sell your company. Let your P.I. license expire. Stop jetting off to play Secret Agent Man, and *then* you can tell me to quit!"

He glared down at her outstretched finger. "Don't be ridiculous. I have employees, people counting on me. Who counts on you, a bunch of spoiled college kids who skip art classes anyway?"

She let her finger drop and straightened to her full five-foot-two height. His angry blue eyes glared down at her but she held her ground. "I count on myself."

She walked to her door and opened it with quiet dignity. "If you'll excuse me, I have more important things to do than argue with a man who obviously has no clue what matters to me."

Rick stomped out. "Fine! Waste your life slaving away for these ingrates in this dingy cubicle. At least with me, you would have been living life instead of studying it."

"Ha!" she called after him. "You haven't been living life any more than I have."

Shoot, that hadn't come out right, and he had left her.

Her cynical American half had known all along he'd leave. But the poor, naive Michiko part buried deep inside had gone and fallen in love with that jerk and chosen this extremely inopportune moment to grieve his loss.

"What happened here?" Holly had come back from her trip to the butt-hut. Meg's eyes blurred and she found herself sobbing into the smoky shoulder of her student assistant's combat jacket.

RICK DROPPED his luggage onto the foyer floor and closed the condo door behind him. His additional week in Hong Kong had netted solid evidence for his client's patent infringement case as well as a nice bonus for his services.

He casually glanced at the answering machine. Five messages. Pressing the play button, he drummed his fingers through three messages from his grandmother, who'd forgotten he was in Hong Kong although he'd called her every day. One message from his sister, who was still in Europe. One message from Nigel bugging him yet again about the pillow book.

No message from Meg. Rick moved through his coming-home routine without much enthusiasm, the condo quiet and musty. Eventually, he made it to the couch in his bathrobe, cold beer in hand where he made some final notes on his laptop.

He tried to drum up the adrenaline rush that accompanied the successful end of a case, but after a long flight back from L.A., the rush fizzled into a trickle.

Rolling his head to stretch his tired muscles, he decided to blame his fatigue on jet lag. Never mind that he'd had a two-day visit to his parents at their vacation house in Santa Barbara and should have ditched any lingering travel effects by now.

That had been an unsettling time. He'd originally only stopped over at his grandmother's urgings. During one of her more fragile moments, she'd become very upset at the possibility that his father's health was declining and no one had seen him in person to be able to tell her the truth. So he'd offered to see for himself after his Hong Kong trip.

Physically, his father was a little weak, but nothing unexpected after open-heart surgery. Emotionally, his dad acted like someone who'd seen the light at the end of the tunnel and wasn't sure if it was the Pearly Gates or a locomotive bearing down on him. To-do lists and self-help books had been scattered over every end table in the house.

Rick would have scoffed at this evidence of belated self-improvement if one short list hadn't caught his eye as it fell to the floor. The only item had been "Tell my wife every single day that I love her."

And there had been a cautious hopefulness between his parents. He'd even seen his dad kiss his mom's hair as she sat reading a novel.

If his parents could start over, why not he and Meg? Had he botched things beyond repair?

He stared at his cell phone. One touch on the number pad and Meg would answer. Or maybe not. Calling her an office lady was pretty unforgivable, as he found out when she got the saddest look he'd ever seen on her face and shown him the door.

He jumped up and rested his forehead on the cool window. The lake was turning inky black as the sun set far to the west. Why had he said that? He'd meant well, wanting to take her away from her frustrating work situation. Traveling with him, living in sunny Southern California, and being free to work whenever she wanted sounded ideal to most women.

But not to Meg. She loved her teaching job, hated L.A. and worked as hard as he did.

She was right. He thumped the window frame with his fist. If she'd been foolish enough to accept his offer, she would have become little more than a…geisha, like those in the pillow book.

The pillow book caught his eye, the antique paper creamy against the dark wood dining table. He walked over and opened it. Seeing the beautiful black-haired women in sensual abandon was a sock in the gut, but he made himself flip the pages. Meg had called it a manual to help newlyweds adjust to their new relationship. At this point, he needed a self-help manual, even if it was two hundred years old.

He turned to the final page and stopped. Here was the painting he'd been looking for, where the man wore a different expression than in the other pictures. Instead of being bored or lecherous, he smiled down at the woman.

Rick knew that smile. He'd seen it reflected on his own face as he made love to Meg in the bathroom. He'd also seen it reflected in store windows as he and Meg walked down the street holding hands. He'd had this picture on his mind while eating Chinese takeout with Meg, but had been too chicken to bring up any of his deepest feelings.

More than desire, more than mere fondness. He blew out a shaky breath. Love? He said it aloud to make it more real. "Love. I love her."

He grinned like a lunatic. It was real. Now all he had to do was convince her.

13

"HOLLY?" MEG STEPPED into the hallway. Her assistant was returning from the drinking fountain, wiping her mouth. "You don't have to stick around since I need to work on those paintings." She'd certainly made up for lost work time in the past week since her fight with Rick. When she'd told him she didn't want to see him again, he'd apparently taken her at her word and hadn't called.

"You still have that *shunga* collection?" Holly had eagerly paged through the erotic drawings, in between surfing the Internet and designing tattoos for her friends.

Meg saw Nigel lurking nearby and beckoned Holly into her office. He'd already bugged her enough about getting Rick to sell the pillow book. "No, Rick has that at his condo." She'd asked Rey to return it. She couldn't keep it now that they'd broken up, and reading margin notes about Lady Miyamoto's wonderful marriage only made her cry.

Meg plastered on a bright smile. "Tonight I have to refine the text translations of the plum-blossom haiku scrolls and the verses inked on the painting of Mt. Fuji."

"Don't stay too late." Holly peered at her through her thick black bangs. "Get some rest. You look like hell."

"Thanks." Meg felt like hell, but it was demoralizing to realize she looked awful, too.

"Sorry, Meg." Holly looked embarrassed. "Only someone who knows you can tell. You're a bit pale, that's all."

"I promise I won't stay long."

"Have security walk you to the campus bus stop." Holly slapped her forehead. "Now I sound like my mother. Or yours."

"Once she knows Rick and I split, she'll start sending me more e-mail photos." Meg rubbed her aching temples. "I don't think I can stand it."

Her assistant wiggled her navy-blue polished fingertips. "I've got a mean mouse finger. I'll delete them for you."

"Thanks, Holly."

Casting one last worried look at her, Holly shut the office door behind her. Meg immersed herself in the soothing haiku, letting the language's archaic formality flow over her jangled nerves. No love poems, no body parts disguised as plants, only serene words devoted to the relentlessness of nature.

Whenever memories threatened her composure, she shoved them to the depths of her mind. Her uncle Yoshi, a student of Zen Buddhism, used to tell her to release her pain in order to attain enlightenment. Did burying pain count? If so, Meg could expect enlightenment at any moment.

She hoped this wasn't all she had to look forward to in the next few decades. Some of her older female professors from grad school had worn their solitude proudly, almost bragging about what they'd passed up to develop their careers—husbands, children, close friendships.

And what did all that professional achievement get you in the end? A scholarship named after you if anyone even cared and a bland writeup in the faculty obit section.

A career wouldn't bring her pink cherry blossoms or kiss her good-night. She blinked hard and sighed, resolving to think really hard about her choices when she wasn't already worn out and lonely.

Two hours later, Meg finished translating the scrolls. She stood and stretched her aching shoulders, shutting off the small desk lamp to give her eyes a rest.

Footsteps sounded in the hallway. The cleaning crew had already finished for the night. Who was it?

The steps stopped at her office and the doorknob slowly turned. Oh no! She knew better than to leave her door unlocked when she worked late. She crouched between the filing cabinet and the dark window, forcing her breath into silence.

"Bloody hell…she told that secretary the book was here. Where the devil is it?" Nigel's exasperated tones echoed through her office as he pawed around her desk. He must have felt her irate glare on his back because he flipped on her desk lamp and turned to face her.

"Ah. Good evening, Megan." He assumed a suave manner, as if he hadn't scared the crap out of her by sneaking into her office.

"Nigel, what are you doing here?" She stalked toward him.

His nose twitched like a white rabbit. "I saw your light and was concerned about your safety."

Her lamp had been turned off. "I'm perfectly fine, Nigel. I'll lock the door when you go. Have a good evening." She herded him to the door.

"Wait!" He dug in his heels. "Megan, please."

"Nigel, what is it?" He looked terrible, beads of sweat running down his temples and dark circles under his eyes.

"That book of *shunga*. I need it."

"The pillow book? Why?" Had he been trying to steal it?

His words tumbled out. "I talked to Dr. Hideo Yamamoto from NYU. As a world expert on Japanese erotic art, he's thrilled to see it. He is only stopping over on his way to the West Coast. I'd have to take the pillow book to his hotel room near O'Hare Airport. I couldn't ask you to meet a strange man in a hotel room, of all places."

Yeah, look at what had happened the last time she had a hotel rendezvous. But she doubted Dr. Yamamoto from NYU was within a thousand miles of Chicago. And there was that little bit about her breakup with Rick. "I don't have the pillow book. It's at the owner's condo."

"You don't have access to the book?" He looked stricken.

"No, I finished my research and Mr. Sokol took it back." Close enough.

His eyes took on a cunning gleam. "I seem to remember he had quite the eye for you. I'd wager that if you called him tonight, you could convince him to give you the book again. Then I can take it to Dr. Yamamoto."

"Convince him?" He wasn't stooping to those depths, was he?

"An extremely personal approach might work." He wiggled his pale eyebrows, his skeletal finger itching to dial Rick's number for her booty call.

"No."

"Don't say 'no' yet," he warned her. "I have great influence with the tenure committee—"

"Screw the tenure committee, screw this department and screw you, Nigel!" The only person *not* screwed would be Rick, the biggest loss of all. "I am not some serf, some lackey, some *office lady* to pimp out so you can get your mitts on a valuable piece of artwork. What do you want it for? Yourself? To sell to pay off your bills?"

He gasped. "What do you know about that?"

"Everybody knows, Nigel. And I intend to show a copy of this department's budget to the dean. Inflated printing estimates, strange expenditures, the whole nine yards!"

"If you do, I'll make you extremely sorry." He balled his fists.

Meg shifted into a matching aggressive stance. "Get out, Nigel." He glared at her and left the room.

Embezzlement and art theft. Loneliness and isolation. What a nice career she'd chosen. She locked her door and called campus security.

Blowing the whistle on her boss might blow her chance for tenure, but the hell with it. Without Rick, tenure didn't mean much to her anyway.

14

"Are you sure you have the space for this?" Rick muscled a small dresser with an attached mirror into his grandmother's bedroom. He winced as his elbow banged into a ceramic lamp. But she had insisted on having this piece of furniture in her new apartment, and it hadn't been a big deal to dismantle it and bring it over in the SUV.

"Of course, Radek." She gave him a coy smile. "You remember when my mother gave me this vanity table. She said every new wife should have a place to make herself pretty for when her husband comes home."

He froze. Grandma was getting more confused every week, and now she thought he was his grandfather. She was looking at him expectantly. He sighed and gave her a hug. "You've always been pretty."

She giggled. "What kind of *kolackies* do you want with your coffee? I have apricot, poppyseed, raspberry and prune."

"One of each, please, except prune." Although he felt ancient thanks to losing Meg, at least he didn't need the extra fiber. Now *that* was something to look forward to.

His grandmother left him in the bedroom and he heard her humming in the kitchenette. He tried to snap himself out of his funk. The vanity table wasn't going to move itself. He eased it into the sliver of space his grandmother had indicated and bolted the mirror back on to it.

He slid an empty drawer back into its slot, but something caught and scraped. He pulled it out to check and found a corner of paper sticking up behind the yellowing adhesive paper lining the drawer box.

Peeling the contact paper away, he found three old envelopes. Two were addressed in his grandmother's handwriting to his grandfather's military post in Occupied Japan. The third envelope was also addressed to his grandfather, but in an unfamiliar hand.

He was about to call out to his grandmother to show her the envelopes, but stopped. Glancing over his shoulder to make sure she was still puttering in the kitchen, he lifted the flap of the third and peered inside.

Several tissue-like pages covered with Japanese script were folded inside. He inhaled a shocked breath, knowing to his bones that this letter unlocked the mystery of his grandfather's pillow book. With his grandmother's mental abilities declining rapidly, he wasn't about to let her know what he'd found.

That book represented so much loss in his life. First

his grandfather's death, then his grandmother's decline and finally the end of his relationship with Meg.

If only Grandpa were around to advise him on this whole falling-in-love thing. He could almost hear his grandfather's voice urging him to get off his hind end and get the girl. Before he could change his mind—or chicken out—he lifted the phone off the cradle and dialed Meg's apartment.

"Hello?" She was home and sounded tired, too. He started to speak but had to clear his throat from the rush of emotion on hearing her voice again.

"If this is a crank call, I can assure you I've had better."

Grinning at her tart voice, he tucked the heavy black phone under his jaw and sat on the edge of his grandmother's bed. "It's Rick."

Now it was her turn to be silent. He waited a few seconds. "Still there?"

"Yes. What is it, Rick? Do you need a written appraisal of the pillow book for your insurance policy?"

He slapped his forehead, mouthing a curse. Too bad he hadn't thought of that a few days ago when he was moping around. "No. Well, yes, that's a good idea, but that's not why I was calling. I need you to read something for me."

"Are your eyes bothering you?"

"I found a Japanese letter addressed to my grandfather. I don't know what to do with it." He paused. "Meg, please. You're the only person I know who can read the letter to me."

"All right. Maybe this will answer a few questions about how he got the pillow book. Let's meet on neutral ground."

"What time is good for you?"

"I've been trapped at home all weekend working on last minute details for the exhibit."

"Why didn't you work at your office?"

She snorted. "Long story. But I need to get some fresh air. Is there a park nearby?"

"Yeah, a couple blocks away. Let me pick you up."

"No, I'll catch a cab."

"If you're sure." He gave her the address. "I'll see you in an hour." One hour to think of what to say to her, how to let her know what he felt.

"One hour…" Her voice trailed off. "Well, let me go so I can finish here."

"Okay, Meg." He'd let her go for that hour but not any longer.

MEG WALKED into the small park, its green coolness calming after her cab ride across the South Side. Sunbathers lay on towels on a wide expanse of grass while cyclists and joggers sped along the paved path circling the park. Parents pushed children on swings and coaxed them down the slides.

Then Rick was walking toward her and her mind went blank. "Hi, Rick."

"Hi, Meg. Thanks so much for coming."

"You're welcome. I have to admit I'm curious about the letter. Addressed to your grandfather, you said?"

She barely knew what she was saying and hoped she sounded coherent. Rick was so handsome, the golden streaks in his hair brighter and that dimple popping out whenever he smiled. He wore a navy-blue UCLA Bruins shirt over gray shorts, the muscles bunching and relaxing in his firm brown legs.

"Yes, his name is on the envelope in English, but the contents of the letter are in Japanese." He stopped at a bench under a huge oak tree and they sat. "I even brought you gloves." He pulled out a lovely pair of gloves, obviously a relic of when a true lady always wore gloves in public. They would have been white fifty years ago, but had aged to a mellow ivory.

Meg smiled. She'd been in such a tizzy changing her outfit four times that she'd forgotten her gloves. She hoped her snug white halter top and boy-cut denim shorts showed Rick she wasn't moping around in her nightshirt eating ice cream from the carton. "Your grandmother's?"

"Yeah, I told her I needed a pair for a friend."

She smoothed the gloves, admiring the dainty pearl buttons at her wrists. "And what did she say to that strange request?"

"Nothing." He sighed. "Nothing seems strange to her anymore. This afternoon she thought I was my grandfather."

"Oh, Rick." She raised her hand to caress his cheek, but seeing the ivory glove snapped her back to why they were here. She pretended to swat away a bug. "About the letter…"

He pulled a Ziploc bag out of his cargo pocket and handed her the gray envelope inside. "Here it is."

Meg gingerly unfolded the fragile pages. The letter had obviously been written by a woman in a flowing and feminine *hiragana* script. She scanned the first few columns of text. "I'll translate as I go, okay?"

"Sure." He nodded, his expression intense.

"'Dear Radek, I know you cannot read Japanese, but I do not have time to find someone who can write my letter to you in English. My friend who does laundry for the soldiers will let me into your quarters so I can slip this letter and my gift into your army trunk.

"'By the time you find this, I will be married to my father's old friend and traveling to his home in the north. My parents had originally arranged a match with his son, who died on Tarawa.'" Meg grimaced. The battle for the tiny coral atoll had been one of World War II's bloodiest.

"'My parents have become more and more suspicious of my absences. I am afraid of what they would do if they found out about you.

"'Marriage to an older man will never compare to our nights spent together as we recreated the paintings in my family's pillow book. You showed me pleasures I had never even imagined. But the memories I will cherish are the simple ones—your tall, strong body covering mine, your big hands holding my face as you kissed me so tenderly.'" Her voice faltered, memories of making love with Rick threatening her self-control. The moist air around them thickened with tension.

He opened his mouth, but she cut him off, desperate to finish translating before she lost her composure. "'I wish I could have risked everything to marry you as you asked, but I am not strong enough to defy my family and my country. You must be very angry with me, and I am so sorry. As a token of my love, I leave you the collection of *shunga*. I pray to my ancestors that you will meet a wonderful American girl and share the joys of physical love together.'"

Meg's eyes filled, blurring the faded writing even further. She and Rick had shared the joys of physical love, but had gotten stuck there. She blinked hard and wiped tears on her forearm. "'May you have a long life and a thousand blessings. Yours always, Shinako Kobayashi.'"

"Shinako. That was her name?"

"Yes, and her parents named her well. 'Shinako' means 'faithful child.'" But not faithful to Rick's grandfather. Poor girl.

Rick blew out a breath. "Wow. So Grandpa had a Japanese girlfriend."

"More than that—it sounds like he asked her to marry him."

"I could have had a Japanese grandmother." He laughed. "Wonder what that would have been like."

"They feed you lots of treats."

"Not much difference." His smile faded, replaced by a serious expression. "Mcg, I didn't just call you to read this letter to me. We need to talk about us."

"Us?" Her hands tightened around the fragile

paper and she quickly relaxed them. "We had plenty to say, and none of it was good."

"Because we're both in unfamiliar territory. I love you like I've never loved anyone. Do you feel the same?"

She stared at him, stunned. "But Rick, there's so much we have to work out. I live here, you live in L.A.—"

"The hell with all the details." He turned her to face him on the park bench. "Meg, please. How do you feel about me?"

His face showed the kind of vulnerability he'd only previously shown during their lovemaking. "I love you, too. So much." Her tears, already brought to the surface by the heartbreaking letter, spilled down her cheeks. "Oh, I'm going to get the paper wet."

He pulled her into his arms and kissed her. The park noises faded into the background until a bolt of lightning sizzled overhead and they both jumped. She shoved Shinako's letter into the baggie and zipped it into her leather purse.

Rick grabbed her hand. "Come on, we've got to get inside."

Meg followed him through the park as the skies opened, drenching them both. He shouted over the thunderstorm, "I'm parked over here. We can dry off at my grandmother's apartment."

"I can't go looking like this!" Her hair was plastered to her head, her mascara no doubt halfway to her chin.

His gaze was sizzling enough to turn the rain to

steam. "You're right. My bed is the only place you can go looking like that."

She followed his stare and gasped. Her white halter top was almost transparent, showing her pebble-hard nipples and the dark circles of her areolas. She crossed her arms over her breasts.

He stopped and stripped off his wet UCLA shirt. "Put this on." She struggled into the heavy cotton, the shirt reaching to her knees. The rain beaded on his bare shoulders and slicked his auburn chest hair. She barely restrained herself from licking the path of every single raindrop.

"I'll take you home." He boosted her into the SUV and drove to her apartment. During the drive, Meg kept sneaking looks at Rick. He caught her eye once and grinned.

Meg unlocked her door and stood shivering in the cool foyer for a second before realizing Rick was still only in his shorts. "You must be freezing." She stripped off his damp UCLA T-shirt and held it out.

He shook his head. "I want you to warm me up."

"Not yet. Not until we settle what's happened between us." She crossed her arms over her chest, hoping he would say the right words so she wouldn't be the only one desperately in love.

He stared at her solemnly without his usual teasing glint. "I've loved Michiko ever since I met her at the Palmer House."

Meg fought back disappointment. "Michiko is easy to love. She doesn't argue, swear or drink hard liquor."

He trailed his fingers across the nape of her neck. "And then I met Dr. Megan O'Malley and fell in love with her, too."

"I love you, too." Meg pushed her damp hair from her face, lingering doubts still needling her. "But how do I know you want me? Not sweet Michiko, not smart-ass Megan, just me?"

He cupped her jaw with his warm hand and smiled tenderly. "I didn't even know what I was looking for until I met you. You *are* a smart-ass—you know that?"

"Takes one to know one." She was finally able to smile in relief.

"But you're also sweet and kind, helping the women's shelter and feeding all your starving students. Why can't you combine the best of both?"

"Both?" She'd never considered the two compatible. "But some Japanese women are so subservient."

"Like those women in the pillow book who take their pleasure as readily as they give it? Like Lady Miyamoto, who demanded fidelity from her husband and got it? Like Shinako, who risked disownment from her family to be with my grandfather, even for a short time?"

She stroked his cheek. "Are you okay with all of that?" Finding out such intimate details had to be awkward.

He shrugged. "I'm glad he wasn't alone over in Japan, and what he brought back with him may have enhanced his marriage.

"But the important thing was that Grandpa grabbed

life. When Shinako left him, he took a chance and fell in love again." He gestured at them together. "Without that, we wouldn't be here."

"To grab life." Meg pondered his challenge. Accepting a life with Rick meant embracing all of what made her Megan Michiko O'Malley. She had much less to lose than Lady Miyamoto and Shinako. Could she be as brave as they were?

Hai. Yes, she could, especially when she gazed at his beautiful eyes, blue as the ocean and deep as their love. "We'll grab life together. You and I."

Epilogue

"HOLLY!" MEG CALLED from her spacious new corner office, where a light pre-Christmas snow drifted past in the afternoon gloom. "Could you please bring in the spring semester budget before I forget?" Examining budget figures was her least pleasant task, but the department's cash flow was much better now that Nigel wasn't betting on the ponies with university funds. According to federal investigators, Nigel had last been spotted in some island republic with notoriously lax extradition laws.

Thanks to the success of her Asian art exhibit, she had been unanimously offered tenure as well as Nigel's former job. Rick had even given permission to display the cherry-blossom geisha painting as well as the maiden and the enchanted stallion-prince.

"Here ya go!" Holly dumped a large binder on her desk, a smile of unholy glee crossing her face.

"You don't have to be so cheerful about it." Meg quit fussing with her brand-new calculator. "Nice hair." Her assistant had streaked it red and green in honor of the upcoming holiday.

"Thanks. But your fiscal flagellation will have to wait. Rick will be here in five minutes."

"Right." Meg pulled on her heavy wool coat. "Tell me why I need to go to his grandmother's house while the new buyers make a final inspection?"

Holly shrugged. "It's the last time he'll get to see the place before it's sold forever. Bound to be emotional, even for a tough guy like him."

"A tough guy like me still can't get used to this weather." Rick sounded like he had a pillow over his face with his heavy hood and wool scarf. He pushed off the hood, his mahogany hair an adorable mess.

"Hi, honey." Meg grabbed her fleece hat and stood on tiptoe in front of him. He rubbed his cold nose over her cheek and she squealed.

He was curiously silent as they drove to the West Lawn bungalow. Grandma Lida was happily settled in her retirement community, having made several new friends. Despite her smaller kitchen and growing forgetfulness, she still created Sunday dinner masterpieces for Rick and Meg twice a month under their close supervision. One visit had even included Rick's parents, who flew out from California to check on Grandma and meet Meg. They had been surprisingly pleasant despite what Rick had told her about his childhood. He was still skeptical about their ability to get along with each other, but had let go the hurtful feelings he'd been carrying around with him.

Meg lowered the heater's setting from "flames of

hell" to "warm breeze." She was sweating under her heavy coat.

"Trying to freeze me out?" Besides having the heater set as high as it could go, he had the heated seats on full blast.

"You'll get used to the cold eventually. By February, this will seem balmy to you."

He gave her a disbelieving look and turned onto his grandmother's street. Despite his complaining about the weather, the man sure looked mighty sexy in the Irish cable-knit sweater she'd given him for his birthday in November. He stopped at the curb and came around to help her into the house.

"Where's the real estate sign?"

"The agent took it away after the contract was signed."

"Oh." It must have come down before the heavy snowfall a couple weeks ago, since she couldn't see any footsteps. "When are the new owners coming for their final inspection?"

"Pretty soon. I want you to see how the house turned out."

Her boots crunched cautiously on the shoveled, salted steps, her breath puffing a white cloud in the darkening sky.

Rick unlocked the front door and held it open for her. "Come in." He hung her coat on a pale wood rack and shed his own heavy jacket.

"And now, the great unveiling." He flicked a

switch, and a row of recessed lighting shone on a modern, yet comfortable living room.

"Oh, Rick, what a wonderful job." The original oak floors were refinished to a gleaming dark honey color.

She stepped onto a plastic runner extending into the kitchen. "Where did that new furniture come from?" A cream-colored leather couch and maple coffee table sat in place of the gargantuan harvest gold couch Meg had seen on a visit before the renovations began.

"The real estate agent said potential buyers like to see furniture in the house so they can imagine living there."

"It definitely works. I can imagine myself living here." She realized her gaffe and linked her arm through his. "I'm sorry. Seeing your grandmother's house one last time must be hard for you."

He smiled at her, his dimples showing. "Don't be sorry. It's not like we're going to live very far away. Come on, let's see the rest of the house." He caught her hand and led her along the plastic runner to the kitchen. "What do you think?"

The poky little room had become a gleaming gourmet paradise. "Whoever bought this house must be a serious cook."

Rick grinned. "If they aren't, they can learn. The cabinets are maple and the countertops are granite. It has a hidden-panel refrigerator, separate cooktop and double ovens."

"I like the center island." She hopped on it and crossed her legs, pointing one high-heeled leather boot at him. "It's exactly the right height."

"For…cooking?" He rested his hand on her knee and casually crept his fingers under her skirt.

"For heating things up, anyway." She uncrossed her legs, shivering as he stroked the sensitive skin above her thigh-high stocking and wedged his big body between her knees. She was about ready to show him the true meaning of an eat-in kitchen when she remembered they wouldn't be alone for long. "Aren't you expecting the new owners?"

He gave her a wry smile. "Right. Two more stops on our tour." The bathroom across the hall had undergone the same radical changes as the kitchen. A compact whirlpool tub was tucked into the corner, and a separate glass-enclosed shower had a skylight over it.

"Absolutely wonderful." She grabbed his hand. "What's the last stop?"

"Come here." He pulled her into a darkened room and flipped a light switch.

"Rick!" The huge bed from his condo stood in the master bedroom's center. Dozens of pink rose petals were sprinkled across a swath of creamy linens. She turned to look at him and tottered on her boot heels as Rick dropped to one knee.

"Megan Michiko O'Malley, will you marry me? Jeez, try saying that three times fast." He flipped open a black velvet ring box and took a deep breath.

"You mean the world to me, honey. Before we met, I never thought I'd find such a smart, sexy woman who'd show me what I was missing when it came to love. I know I'm a better man because of you, and I want to spend the rest of my life with you."

Meg couldn't say anything. Her brain and voice had lost contact at the sight of a square-cut diamond sparkling in a gold setting.

He took her left hand and kissed her bare ring finger. "I never thought I'd see the day when you were speechless, but you're starting to make me nervous."

"Yes!" She threw her arms around his neck and kissed him hard, swiping her tongue across the roof of his mouth just the way he liked it. He caught her around the waist and staggered to the bed, pulling her on top of him. Meg scooped the ring out of the box. "I love this ring, and I love you."

"Good." He ran his hands under her sweater, flipping open the front clasp to her bra.

She batted his touch away, but not before he'd stroked her nipples to an aching fullness. "Rick, no! I can't believe you'd do this right before those real estate people arrive."

He sprawled onto the bed, laughing uncontrollably. "Meg, Meg, I think the shock has shorted out your magnificent mind. There *are* no real estate people. I remodeled the house, but I never put it on the market. I bought it from my grandmother as a wedding present for us."

"You did all this for us?" She looked around the

beautifully decorated bedroom. "You were pretty sure of yourself."

"I wasn't sure at all. But I took a chance on it, like you took a chance on loving me." He pressed a kiss on her forehead. "Did it work? Will you live with me here?"

"Well…" She pretended to consider his offer, all the while screaming for joy inside.

"I have one more present for you." He opened a drawer in the matching nightstand and lifted out the pillow book.

"Oh, Rick." Since Meg was Japanese-born and a scholar writing the definitive treatise on Lady Miyamoto's pillow book, the Japanese Agency for Cultural Affairs had not pressed for returning the pillow book to Japan. Rick would need to make the book available for occasional exhibition, but that was all.

"I want you to pick out a top-of-the-line, climate-controlled display case for our bedroom. That way, we can keep the paintings safe and keep them close for inspiration. What do you say?" A grin tugged at the corners of his beautiful mouth.

"You've got a deal. A man who appreciates the finer things in life doesn't come along every day."

"I wanted to show you how much I love you." Rick freed a painting from the book.

Meg took the painting, holding it by the edges. The blue-robed man embraced his lover. She lay on a *tatami* mat, her long black hair spilling over his arms as he held her close. Instead of the typically stoic expression often found in the paintings, he gazed down at her tenderly. The woman smiled up at him, her emotions as open to him as her body.

Before she and Rick had fallen in love over the summer, Meg had always skimmed past this painting, the couple's deep sentiments making her slightly uncomfortable.

But now Rick was looking at her with the same loving expression she'd seen on his face every day since. "Read the poem out loud, sweetheart."

Meg blinked away the tears beginning to blur her vision but she already knew the haiku by heart. "'Come to me, my love. Twist your black tresses into rope and bind me to you forever.'" She set the painting on the nightstand and brushed back the lock of hair that had curled on his forehead. "How did you know that the poem uses the word *ai,* romantic love? The other pictures don't mention love at all."

He kissed her hand and set the painting carefully on the nightstand. "I guessed. The couple in the painting looked so much in love that I had your Japanese grad assistant translate it for me." He rolled her underneath him, the crushed rose petals emitting a delicious fragrance. "Whenever I see that painting, I'll think of how much we love each other."

"I love you, too." A giddy gust of laughter welled out of her. "I can't believe you did all this for us. A wonderful house like this deserves an extra-special housewarming party."

He kissed her tenderly, his blue eyes glistening. "I would live in a shack and call it home, as long as you were with me."

Hot tears of happiness ran down the sides of her cheeks as she clutched him tight. She'd come to Chicago to find her place in the world, never expecting to find it in the arms of such a special man.

* * * * *

Happily ever after is just the beginning...

Turn the page for a sneak preview of
DANCING ON SUNDAY AFTERNOONS
by
Linda Cardillo

Harlequin Everlasting—Every great love
has a story to tell.
A brand-new line from Harlequin Books
launching this January!

Prologue

Giulia D'Orazio
1983

I had two husbands—Paolo and Salvatore.

Salvatore and I were married for thirty-two years. I still live in the house he bought for us; I still sleep in our bed. All around me are the signs of our life together. My bedroom window looks out over the garden he planted. In the middle of the city, he coaxed tomatoes, peppers, zucchini—even grapes for his wine—out of the ground. On weekends, he used to drive up to his cousin's farm in Waterbury and bring back manure. In the winter, he wrapped the peach tree and the fig tree with rags and black rubber hoses against the cold, his massive, coarse hands gentling those trees as if they were his fragile-skinned babies. My neighbor, Dominic Grazza, does that for me now. My boys have no time for the garden.

In the front of the house, Salvatore planted roses. The roses I take care of myself. They are giant, cream-colored, fragrant. In the afternoons, I like to sit out on the porch with my coffee, protected from the eyes of the neighborhood by that curtain of flowers.

Salvatore died in this house thirty-five years ago. In the last months, he lay on the sofa in the parlor so he could be in the middle of everything. Except for the two oldest boys, all the children were still at home and we ate together every evening. Salvatore could see the dining room table from the sofa, and he could hear everything that was said. "I'm not dead, yet," he told me. "I want to know what's going on."

When my first grandchild, Cara, was born, we brought her to him, and he held her on his chest, stroking her tiny head. Sometimes they fell asleep together.

Over on the radiator cover in the corner of the parlor is the portrait Salvatore and I had taken on our twenty-fifth anniversary. This brooch I'm wearing today, with the diamonds—I'm wearing it in the photograph also—Salvatore gave it to me that day. Upstairs on my dresser is a jewelry box filled with necklaces and bracelets and earrings. All from Salvatore.

I am surrounded by the things Salvatore gave me,

or did for me. But, God forgive me, as I lie alone now in my bed, it is Paolo I remember.

Paolo left me nothing. Nothing, that is, that my family, especially my sisters, thought had any value. No house. No diamonds. Not even a photograph.

But after he was gone, and I could catch my breath from the pain, I knew that I still had something. In the middle of the night, I sat alone and held them in my hands, reading the words over and over until I heard his voice in my head. I had Paolo's letters.

* * * * *

Silhouette®

ROMANTIC SUSPENSE

Excitement, danger and passion guaranteed!

Same great authors and riveting editorial you've come to know and love.

Look for our new name next month as Silhouette Intimate Moments® becomes Silhouette® Romantic Suspense.

Visit Silhouette Books at www.eHarlequin.com

SIMRS0107

This February...

*Catch NASCAR Superstar **Carl Edwards** in*
SPEED DATING!

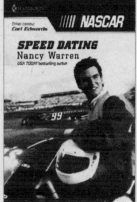

Kendall assesses risk for a living—
so she's the last person you'd
expect to see on the arm of a
race-car driver who thrives on the
unpredictable. But when a bizarre
turn of events—and NASCAR
hotshot Dylan Hargreave—inspire
her to trade in her ever-so-structured
existence for "life in the fast lane"
she starts to feel she might be
on to something!

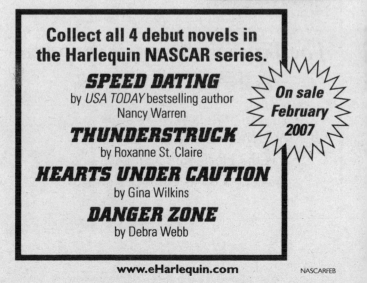

Collect all 4 debut novels in the Harlequin NASCAR series.

SPEED DATING
by *USA TODAY* bestselling author
Nancy Warren

THUNDERSTRUCK
by Roxanne St. Claire

HEARTS UNDER CAUTION
by Gina Wilkins

DANGER ZONE
by Debra Webb

On sale February 2007

www.eHarlequin.com

NASCARFEB

What a month!

In February watch for

Rancher and Protector
Part of the Western Weddings miniseries
BY JUDY CHRISTENBERRY

The Boss's Pregnancy Proposal
BY RAYE MORGAN

Also in February, expect
MORE of what you love
as the Harlequin Romance line
increases to six titles per month.

www.eHarlequin.com   SRJAN07

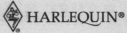

HARLEQUIN®

Blaze™

COMING NEXT MONTH

#303 JINXED! Jacquie D'Alessandro, Jill Shalvis, Crystal Green
Valentine Anthology
Valentine's Day. If she's lucky, a girl can expect to receive dark chocolate, red roses and fantastic sex! If she's not…well, she can wind up with a Valentine's Day curse…and fantastic sex! Join three of Harlequin Blaze's bestselling authors as they show how three very unlucky women can end up getting *very* lucky.…

#304 HITTING THE MARK Jill Monroe
Danielle Ford has been a successful con artist most of her life. Giving up the habit has been hard, but she's kicked it. Until Eric Reynolds, security chief at a large Reno casino, antes up a challenge she can't back away from—one that touches her past and ups her odds on bedding sexy Eric.

#305 DON'T LOOK BACK Joanne Rock
Night Eyes, Bk. 1
Hitting the sheets with P.I. Sean Beringer might have been a mistake. While the sex is as hot as the man, NYPD detective Donata Casale is struggling to focus on their case. They need to wrap up this investigation fast. Then she'll be free to fully indulge in this fling.

#306 AT HER BECK AND CALL Dawn Atkins
Doing It…Better!, Bk. 2
Autumn Beskin can bring a man to his knees. The steamy glances from her new boss, Mike Fields, say she hasn't lost her touch. But while he may be interested in more than her job performance, he hasn't made a move. Guess she'll have to nudge this fling along.

#307 HOT MOVES Kristin Hardy
Sex & the Supper Club II, Bk. 2
Professional dancer Thea Mitchell knows all the right steps—new job, new city, new life. But then Brady McMillan joins her Latin tango dance class and suddenly she's got two left feet. When he makes his move, with naughty suggestions and even naughtier kisses, she doesn't know what to expect next!

#308 PRIVATE CONFESSIONS Lori Borrill
What does a woman do when she discovers that her secret online sex partner is actually her real-life boss—the man she's been lusting after for two years? She goes for it! Trisha Bain isn't sure how to approach Logan Moore with the knowledge that he's Pisces47, only that she wants to make the fantasy a reality. Fast…

www.eHarlequin.com

HBCNM0107